THORNTON STORIES

Also by Dale Boyer (Available from OhBoy Books)

The Dandelion Cloud

Other Titles available from OhBoy Books:

Handschuh, Judith – *No Justice!*
O'Hara, Scot – *Tarantella*

Visit www.OhBoyBooks.com

THORNTON STORIES

TALES OUT OF SCHOOL

———

Dale Boyer

Published by OhBoy Books.

OhBoy Books
400 East Ohio, Suite 1602
Chicago, IL 60611
www.OhBoyBooks.com

ISBN: 0997013427
ISBN 13: 9780997013429

for
all my teachers

and for Scot

TABLE OF CONTENTS

THORNTON STORIES

LICENSE

———•———

S TANDING WITH MY FATHER ONE cold, snowy Christmas Eve beside the dirty, carbon-fumed winter highway, teeth chattering, looking longingly at the cozy yellow, frosted-over lights from our picture window across the frigid, darkened roadway, I stood still while my father attempted to make me a man.

"What's that one?" he demanded, pointing down the icy, headlight-stabbed road in the 20-degree darkness.

I looked into the endless stream of headlights coming toward me, melting in a sea of lights like those upon the Christmas tree inside our warm house.

"A Ford," I said weakly.

"No, no, no. You've got to call them out, make and year, before you can read the license plate," he said. "That's the trick of it. Like this." He pointed to a distant glob of light that wobbled and separated into two, like a cell dividing: "Fifty-eight Chevy." He snapped his fingers, and we watched the car pass by in the silence of his triumph.

"See? Now, what's that one?" he demanded.

Seeing a large car approaching, I made a guess: "Cadillac."

"What year?"

"Fifty-five," I said, purely guessing again.

"No, I think it's a fifty-nine," said my father, watching it approach, then pass. "Yes sir, fifty-nine it is. See that rear end? They stopped making rear ends like that after the fifty-nines came out."

"Oh," I said, afraid he was going to ask me to guess another one, but he didn't.

"You get good at it after a while," he said, half-heartedly.

In his overcoat and top hat, my father looked like what I imagined a KGB spy would look like. I'd been reading about them lately: they were everywhere after the recent Cuban missile crisis: imposters masquerading as decent American citizens, the way I was masquerading interest in dad's game or, on a larger level, I guess, the way I was masquerading at being a man, when all I really wanted was to go inside and sit beneath the tinseled glow of the Christmas tree and experience what my dad undoubtedly would have labeled the more "feminine comforts" inside. I was gearing up to have to endure the ordeal a great while longer -- such trials were common with my father; but, abruptly, he said: "Well, let's go back inside the house now."

I knew my father was disappointed, but, I was cold and didn't care and, in some way, I knew he didn't care about me so much as he felt let down by the kind of boy I had become.

Failure: that was the gift I remember giving my father that Christmas.

———

My father was Vice President of the Thornton State Bank and Trust, a small-town operation in the nowhere town of Thornton, Illinois, population 5,700. Add Thornton College, the local school, to the count, and that was good for maybe another 500. In other words, he was a big duck in a little pond. My father was the kind of man who was everyone's friend and no one's: he could glad-hand everybody out at the local greasy spoon, act like the big cheese, schmooze the guys down at the courthouse and City Hall, help people out with loans he "personally" approved at the bank, and yet, nobody really liked him. I'm not even sure Mom really did; but, being the wife of a Vice President did carry a lot of privilege in a town as small as Thornton, and I know Mom appreciated that. People knew who she was, and were deferential, if for no other reason than her husband held their mortgage at the bank. But, that's not gratitude or friendship: it's fear. Because my dad worked at basically the only operation in town, he knew the score on everyone: who was behind on their mortgage, who'd had a bumper crop the year before, whose farm was in trouble. He was nominally -- though not directly -- in charge of repossessions, too; so, often, we found ourselves driving a nearly new car, or boat, courtesy of someone else's misfortune. We also drove a series of new RV homes with amazing regularity, simply because my father always had the inside scoop on someone else's bad debt. Since then, I can only speculate what kind of animosity it must have engendered in a town of 5,700, to see my dad and our family constantly showing up in something "new" which, perhaps, used to belong to them. And yet, it was a hard-working farming community, and I think most people had enough of that hard-boiled, Midwestern sense of justice ingrained in them to know that if they failed in making payments on something, they were naturally going to lose the title on it, just as surely as the crops would fail if the rains didn't come.

The first time I ever encountered my father's car, parked ticking and warm, in the shadows of the parking lot of the Bella Vista Motel on the outskirts of town at 2:30 on a Tuesday afternoon, I didn't know what to think. Despite the amazing rapidity of vehicles my father had gone through over the years, there was no mistaking his car. At that point, he was driving a champagne-colored Cadillac with white-walled tires (to this day, and to my father's utter chagrin, I'm sure, I do not know what model type and year); but, it looked like no other set of wheels anywhere in town. My first thought was that it was possible my father was meeting someone for a business lunch; and yet, this was not a place where one would have a meeting with a client: there was no restaurant or diner of any kind attached -- it was just a roadside motel located at the furthest limits of the town, just before the corn-fields began in earnest. All I could conclude was that he was having an affair with someone, and all I could feel was anger. Even if he could (and did) boss everyone around in this podunk town in the middle of Illinois -- repossess their cars and hold their mortgages over them -- still, how could he possibly think it was okay to carry on like this in the middle of the day in such a small town, to betray Mom in this totally outrageous fashion? Had he no shame at all? What gave him the right?

The only time I can ever remember *not* letting my father down -- the single, incontrovertible memory I have as a youth of meeting his approval -- was when I unexpectedly did well in a junior high school "Punt, Pass, and Kick" competition. Before this, there had been the miseries of Little League where, despite my father's prominence in town, I was never good enough to play any other position besides right field; the agonies of Boy Scout Pinewood Derbies where, despite my father's endless hours in the garage, tooling and retooling my soapbox car, my roadster never came in better than third; the endless practices for basketball, where I could hear my father over all the others in the gym, or even -- most embarrassing of all -- conferring with, and haranguing, the coaches as to why they didn't put me in. My father hadn't even wanted to take me to the football competition, fearing, I think, that I would ultimately be a disappointment, as in everything else public connecting me to him so far. Indeed, I was everything my father was not: shy, bookish. I greatly preferred not talking to others if given the opportunity -- something my father could never have imagined, since, as he often said, "You never know what someone might be able to do for you until you talk to them."

Indeed, I can't even recall what possessed me to enter the competition after so many other failures: perhaps a sense of misguided hope? A desire to emulate and impress Kevin Treadle? Kevin was a classmate and idol of mine who lived, interestingly and provocatively, in the poorer, more run-down part of town, and whose sense of pure joy and effortlessness in everything he did was my secret and endless fascination. I knew Kevin was trying out, too, and had even seen him practicing with his friends; I watched him as frequently and surreptitiously as I could. At any rate, I was hell-bent on entering the contest, and it was only at the last moment, and reluctantly, that my father had deigned to be on hand.

I can still remember the astonishment -- both his and mine -- as I released all my pent-up frustration and anger, and kicked the football out into the sky-blue, summer air high above the pine trees surrounding the high school field. The football made an arc so perfect and spectacular we were both left absolutely speechless. It was as though the whole world stopped to watch; and, as the football landed at the other end of the field, bouncing wildly about, my father was already running onto the field before it settled, the incredulity and enthusiasm spilling from him as he was all over me, slapping me and saying: "That was *amazing*, son," (this was also the only time I remember him addressing me as "son;" usually, it was "boy"). "I would *never* have dreamed in a million years you had that in you!" And then, almost immediately -- pathetically and predictably -- the litany began as my father enlisted the support of all the others on the field: all the ones whose financial straits he was intimately aware of, the ones whose boats or trailers he may just recently have repossessed, imploring them all: "Can you *believe* that? Wasn't that just the most amazing goddamned thing you ever saw?"

Sadly, the experience was not to be repeated: I never even came close to equaling that level of performance in any other parts of the competition. Indeed, when asked to repeat that unaccountably perfect kick -- whether from choking on the pressure of the watching eyes, or due to some deep-seated, unconscious resentment of my father and a desire to see him (for once, at least) not get exactly what he wanted -- each subsequent attempt I made at the ball came up short. But, I had done so well in the punting phase that my average scores in the other areas led me to take second place in the competition overall.

In the months immediately following, my father's energies quickly shifted into finding a way for me to become the next Joe Namath; but, no amount of football gear or practice kicking nets or any of the other paraphernalia he acquired in the increasingly desperate pursuit of his dream paid off. Bemused by my failure, my father would sometimes make passing reference to the competition: "I have to believe you've got it in you, son -- that kick of yours that day wasn't just an anomaly." Yet, that, indeed, seemed to be exactly what it had been. He also invoked this often when discussing my seeming inability to follow in his footsteps at the bank, saying, "You're just not *applying* yourself. If you really put your mind to it, like that day out on the football field, you'd see what you could accomplish. You just don't *want* to, is all. Sometimes I think you *want* to make me look bad."

One day, after my high school graduation, when most of the summer had passed (I would have gone to college, but my father had put the kibosh on that idea, insisting that he needed me to stay on in town, to be his "right-hand man"), feeling particularly inept and useless in the role of "Collections Agent" which my father was trying to hammer me into at the bank, I had a revelation. I had witnessed now, for weeks, the spectacle of my father's unmistakable vehicle parked blatantly and unapologetically in the shade on the faded blacktop of the Bella Vista Motel, when suddenly I realized: if my father could carry on this way; if he thought he had the right to act as though he were invisible -- as though there weren't a soul in Thornton who could touch him -- I would call him at his game. After all, I even knew who she was now: I'd seen them coming back one afternoon, my father dropping her off at the local breakfast shop a few blocks down from the bank, just the way you'd do if you were giving somebody a simple lift somewhere. She was really a loose piece: divorced twice, she ran a little card shop just off the square. Over the years, I'd heard it said she'd sleep with anyone. Now, apparently, that anyone included my father.

Heading back to Main Street, I parked my car illegally (I did it often now because -- after all -- being my father's son, who in this town was going to ticket *me*?) in front of the Greek Revival columns of the Thornton State Bank and Trust, its square face looking blandly out across the red-bricked square, its silent and emasculated canons rusting in the center of the vacant park, and the flag up on the flagpole flapping listlessly. I headed up the concrete stairs, swung back the glass door to the cool and unaccustomed feel of air conditioning inside the tall, reverberating lobby, walked up to Gretta, who was seated behind the 1930s grill and said, "Hey, Gretta. Do you know where my father is?"

"Hey, Greg," said Gretta, who had been a fixture at the bank since World War II. Swiveling around on her stool to address a girl farther back in the room, she said, "Alice, do you know if Mr. Swenson is around?"

Through the glass, I could hear the tinny, muffled patter as she and Alice tried to decide whether my father was, or wasn't, in the building.

Turning back at last, Gretta said, "We think he's still out at lunch, hon."

"Hmm," I said, affecting the best, most innocent brand of nonchalance I could manage. "I passed his car out at the Bella Vista a little while ago. You think he's still there?"

"You passed it *where*?" said Gretta, leaning in closer to the glass to hear better.

"The Bella Vista Motel? Is he doing some kind of deal out there?"

"I wouldn't know, hon," said Gretta, looking vaguely flustered. "You want to wait for him in his office?"

"Sure," I said. "Don't mind if I do."

And so, I sat for over an hour in his office -- the fox making himself comfortable in the hen house -- waiting to ambush him. When he walked in at last, his clothes all newly retucked, tie freshly retied, trying to look as though he'd merely been out drawing contracts for new acreage some farmer had just recently purchased, he began to putter about in the office, then jumped as he spied me on his big leather couch in the shadows of the room.

"Greg, what are you doing in here?"

"The question is," I said, enjoying the sight of catching him off guard: "What are you doing out at the Bella Vista Motel?"

My father looked at me exactly the way a not-very-experienced child looks when he tries to tell his first lie, and I wondered suddenly how he'd ever made it at the bank. He wasn't that sharp after all -- certainly not if this episode was any indication.

"Oh, just out on a social call," my father said. "Why? You saw me there?"

"Today, and once or twice a week for the past few months. That's an awful lot of socializing, isn't it, Dad?"

"Now, look here," said my dad. "I don't know what you're trying to imply..."

"Oh, save it, Dad," I said. "Why don't I just call up the front desk at the Bella Vista and ask them what your name on the register there might imply?"

"Look, boy, I don't know what your game is," said my father slowly, "but, what gives you the right to come in here and start accusing me --"

"The *right*?" I interrupted him. "You're a fine one to talk about 'rights.' What gives you the right to carry on behind Mom's back? What gives you the right to park your car right out in broad daylight every afternoon where everybody in the whole fucking town can see it?"

My father flinched at this, as though the thought had never even occurred to him that he might have been observed. Great license does that sometimes, I guess: it makes one feel invulnerable.

"Okay, okay," said my father at last. "But, you don't understand: I love her."

"Oh, Christ!" I said. "You can't be serious."

"I *am*," said my father, indignantly. "We want to get married someday. I'm going to ask your mother for a divorce."

I was stunned. "Oh, sure," I said. "You trade everything else in on a regular basis, so why not Mom?"

"You're awfully fresh," said my father, looking at me, startled.

"Yeah, and from what I hear, she ain't."

My father looked at me narrowly. "What the hell are you talking about? How do you even know who she is?"

"Are you an idiot?" I said. "*Everybody* knows. We're the laughingstock of the town."

My father looked at me levelly, then said: "No, son, that would be *you*."

I'd been acting like I was the one with all the cards; but, now I saw my father the way he'd be in a negotiation: nasty as the rattlers you stumbled on sometimes out in the middle of the cornfields. Still, I could be a real shit, too.

"What I don't get," I ventured, as boldly as I dared, "is, why the hell would you marry her? Nobody else seemed to feel the need to."

My father paused, the outrage building in him. "Where the hell do you get off saying that to *me* -- you, who've never acted like a man in your whole god-damned life?"

"Oh, and you're *such* a great man," I said, mustering all the sarcasm I could. "What did you do to make her sleep with you? Call in the loan on her shop?"

My father stood now, all five-foot-six-and-a-half inches of pudgy, well-fed privilege. "Well, I see my son's finally getting some balls after all this time. Where've they been all these years, is what I want to know? But, I've got news for you, kiddo. You've got a lot to learn if you think you can talk to me that way in *this* town. I've worked my ass off my whole life so I can do whatever the hell I want, say whatever I want *to* whoever I want, and yes, even fuck whoever I want. And there's not anybody, including you, who's going to tell me any different. You think you got anything on me, kiddo? You've got a lot to learn, about *both* me and your mother. Now, get out!" he bellowed. "Get out, and re-member: you try to pull any shit on me and I'll be so far up your ass you'll be seeing double."

I wasn't sure where to go or what to do after that. After all, there were exactly two main streets in town. So, you either headed towards the bank and the square at the center, or perpendicularly away from it; everything else was just cornfields. Cowed after this encounter, I walked like an automaton to my car, heading just anywhere away from the bank and through the downtown. Then, I changed my mind, not wanting to dip down into the hollow where I would eventually have to pass the loathsome Bella Vista Motel. Instead, I hung a left and headed over to the main residential area on the east side. For a while, I'd been sort of dating Kevin Treadle's sister, Carol Ann, though my heart wasn't really much in it. In truth, I'm not really sure what my heart *was* in lately. My father never failed to comment on the fact that Carol Ann's and Kevin's house was in a less affluent section ("Why the hell you couldn't take up with one of the Sykes girls or, at the very least, someone who lived in the New Edition, I'll never understand"). Thinking about it, I thought perhaps the answer was contained within the question: anything I could do to piss off my father in any way, so much the better.

As I pulled up in front of Carol Ann's yard, denuded by their two large dogs, the driveway filled up with one rusted pickup that never seemed to go anywhere, and her youngest brother's much banged-up, faded, pink-and-yellow Hot Wheels, I found myself seeing Carol Ann's family though my father's eyes: there certainly was not a lot that signified promise or potential here. Still, Kevin seemed to be making a pathway out: since graduation, he had been taking classes at Sangamon State -- an option I'd enviously explored with my father after he'd said no to full-blown college, but which he'd nixed as well ("Hell, I can teach you everything you need to know").

Catching sight of me through the open screen door, Carol Ann leaned out and said, "How come you never call before you come over first?"

So, I could see she was starting in on me right away.

"I got to call to come see my girlfriend?" I said, looking more put out than I actually felt.

"I'm your 'girlfriend' whenever you don't have noplace else to go," said Carol Ann, still holding the laundry basket, and looking torn between holding onto it to prove her point, and setting it down to be free to take advantage of whatever diversion I might have planned. "Besides, half the time I'm not sure if you're here to see me or Kevin."

This stung a bit because, in truth, I had, indeed, been scanning the yard for any sign of him.

"Come on," I said, trying to cover up the awkwardness her accuracy had provoked. "Let's blow this hole for a while." I wasn't sure what we were going to do, but I wanted at least to get outside the limits of the town so I could clear my head.

"Can't," said Carol Ann. "I got to watch my little brother."

"Where's your mom?"

"She's out at the 4-H getting stuff ready for the bake sale this weekend."

"Where's Kevin?" I said, nervous about asking this, given what she'd just said.

"At his class."

"Shit," I said, hanging my head and seeing no way around it: we were stuck here until someone came and relieved her of the obligation of watching Tommy.

"Well, come on in. We can watch TV anyway."

Sitting beside her reluctantly on the dilapidated sofa, its light-brown color so faded it was almost tan, its shape somewhere between square and oval, and its arms and back covered with a light down of both cat and dog hair, I saw that we were going to be frustrated again. Her brother, Tommy, lay on his stomach in front of the TV wearing a cowboy hat, eating a PopTart and drinking a glass of lemonade in a posture that reminded me of Kevin's freewheeling nature, some-how. The TV set was loudly blaring cartoons.

"Can't we at least change the station?" I said, after we had endured several inane minutes of *Scooby Doo.*

"I'm watching this," said Tommy, turning around to look at us with just enough hint of Kevin's features to make me feel guilty once more.

Carol Ann shrugged, and I sat there for a moment, thinking: "Christ, what a predicament." I reached out after a moment and rubbed Carol Ann's legs, not so much because I wanted to, but because I supposed I could: she was my girlfriend, after all, wasn't she? Didn't that give me the right?

Carol Ann slapped my hand away. "Don't," she said, shyly at first, indicating her brother in front of us.

"He can't see us," I whispered into her ear, more just stating the obvious than from any real desire to be covert. I let a few minutes go by. Then, thinking about my father and his piece of ass out at the Bella Vista -- and probably Kevin, too, with whatever possible new girlfriend he had -- I reached up and decided I was going to assert my rights as well by touching her breast. Immediately, Carol Ann went electric with disapproval, slapping my hand away and saying, "Stop it!"

"What the hell?" I said, trying not to look at Tommy, who had turned around now and was looking at us with Kevin's questioning eyes.

"Your daddy may own everyone and everything in this town," said Carol Ann, "but you don't own me, and you never will."

"Fine," I said, surprised and humiliated by this second confrontation of the day, but feeling, in some deep, dark part of me, that the situation had been building to this point for quite some time. "You might have let me know you felt like this before today."

"Anybody else but you would have seen it!" said Carol Ann, her face quivering with contempt. "You can't just show up here whenever you feel like it, cop a feel, and then forget about me the whole rest of the time. Anyway, you're a high school graduate now, you're supposed to be an adult. So, what the hell are you doing still hanging around here?"

"Fuck if I know," I said, feeling ostracized and confused, the intent to wound building inside me before I really had time to think about what I was saying: "My daddy's right about you and your family: none of you are ever going to amount to shit."

"Well, ain't *that* the pot calling the kettle black," said Carol Ann, standing now and pointing toward the door, furious. "Get the hell on out of here, you spineless little twerp. Go kiss your daddy's ass, because you sure as hell ain't ever going to get anywhere near mine."

———•———

After that I just drove: out past the high school with its crooked pines and air of stifling defeat (a sad sign still proclaiming, as if proudly: "Home of the 1958 State Semi-Finalists" -- a sight which Kevin Treadle may have left behind, but I had not), out past Sykes' Horse Plantation with its two faux, Greek Revival columns on the porch and its black, wrought-iron lantern tied down heavily -- like everything else in this town -- by four thick, ugly chains. After a while, though, I finally stopped. All around me, the gravel roads spread out through the cornfields toward the sky, and there I was, dead center in the middle, in more ways than one.

I pulled over to the side of the road into some hempy weeds and, once the car had stopped, I could hear the hum of the earth, the occasional cricket or insect, or the chirp of a bird. A tractor was thrumming off somewhere, and I just sat for a moment, feeling the August heat start to radiate in on me, and the reverberating quiet. Ahead, I could see two blue silos in the distance ("Always look to see how many silos a farmer has," my dad always said, "to let you know how well-off he is"). Leave it to him always to be looking for the angle. I didn't know this farm or these people, but they looked to be doing well. And me? Well, I was sitting on an unmarked road at the edge of a one-horse town in a nowhere state after I'd just pissed off my girlfriend *and* my father, and there was nothing, apparently, I could do about any of it. I was, myself, ensiled.

Later, after heading all the way into Springfield, a little under an hour away, I sat outside the bar for a while, just looking at it, before I decided to go in. I have to say, I'd thought about coming here many times before. I'd even scoped it out a time or two. But, I was afraid about what actually entering the bar would say about me as a person -- afraid that, once I did go in, the course of everything from there on was irreversible. It was the middle of the day, not many people were around, and it was shameful, of course, to be going into a place like this. *What the hell*, I thought after a moment. *Didn't I have the right?*

As I entered the darkness, it took my eyes a full minute or so to adjust to the different light inside and, after my sight had cleared, I made my way, stiff-legged, up to the bar, as if the eyes of everybody in the world were watching me give in to this unforgivable impulse -- to this certain, slow, departure on the path to dissolution and debauchery. I ordered a beer from the dark-haired, very tan bartender, and sat there, nervous and self-conscious, until at last I steeled myself to look around the place. A few small groups of men sat here or there together in the booths, but none of them looked up at me as if I were a freak. And, why should they? After all, they were in here for the same reason I was, so why should I be worried?

In a little while, a man walked in and sat down next to me -- kind of a big, nice-looking guy. I was a little uncomfortable that he'd sat down right beside me, when every other barstool in the place was empty. After he sat, he ordered a beer and, looking at my nearly empty glass, said, "Can I buy you a drink?"

"Sure, I said, feeling suddenly self-conscious again. I wasn't even 21 yet -- shouldn't even really be in here -- and yet, here I was, not only drinking in the middle of the day, but accepting a drink from a total stranger.

We got to talking as the time wore on. After a while, the guy put his hand on my knee, and I just sat there for a moment, allowing it. *Well, there it is*, I thought, guessing this was it, at last: the moment, the decision point, the whatever. I had the vague, dull sense there was something I should be objecting to, and yet, in some ways, everything about it seemed perfect and unexpected, like that football I'd kicked away from me that day: clean and clear and somehow absolutely right. It was such a different feeling from all the other times it *hadn't* felt that way -- nights like that cold December evening when I'd stood beside my father, trying to identify these things that kept on flying up at me out of the goddamned dark.

RUNAWAY

———◆———

I ALWAYS THOUGHT I'D BE THE one to run away from Thornton someday, instead of getting left holding the bag. I suppose I shouldn't be surprised: my father was a double-dealer in absolutely every sense of the word; so, why should it have come as any kind of shock to us that he wound up double-crossing everyone -- that, in the end, *he* ran away, and we were the ones left behind?

My father had been carrying on an affair for several years -- an affair I'd caught wind of, and which, I'm sure, many other people in the town were aware of as well. Still, I never really thought he'd follow through and marry the woman, who owned a small shop in town. Thornton was so small, his affair couldn't have been a secret from many; indeed, I'd actually confronted him about it myself, and that's when he told me he planned to marry the woman. Still, I thought this was just so much smoke and mirrors, as was so often the case with my father, especially since -- shortly after this confrontation -- he'd taken my mother with him on a trip to St. Louis to interview for a bank position there. I took this as a sign he'd finally come to his senses, and was going to try to patch things up with Mom, start anew; but, this was just another false illusion where my father was concerned (just about all of my illusions concerning my father were false -- except, perhaps, the bad ones).

What my father did, in fact, was play us all for fools. Instead of taking my mother with him as an attempt to break off the affair, move away and begin again with mom, his actual purpose in having her accompany him was to present a notion of complete and total marital bliss and harmony to his new employers -- show them what a stable, solid, family man he was -- so he could get the job. Once this had been achieved, and the position had been secured (with my mother's unwitting help), he promptly announced to my mother and me that he was, simultaneously, accepting the position in St. Louis, moving out of town and, unceremoniously divorcing mom to marry his new wife, Gwen.

Of course, I can't tell you how flabbergasted we both were, especially Mom. Given my father's previous behavior for -- really -- his entire life, though, we should have seen it coming: he had always, more or less, done whatever he wanted to do, traded in this or that car or boat or house whenever he felt like it; so, why should trading in his wife and family have been any different?

After the initial shock had worn off, and he had moved away with Gwen, Mom and I tried to carry on as best we could. I had already moved out of the house; so, not having my dad around wasn't that new to me. For my mom, however, who had more or less established her identity in town as being the wife of a bank Vice President, the adjustment was very hard. Not only was there the initial shock to get over; but then, in such a small town, the fallout of knowing that her husband had run off with another woman was a stigma my mother found hard to bear. In truth, my father had never been well-liked, so there was a lot of immediate support and sympathy for my mom ("How that man could just run off and abandon you like that -- especially with a woman like her!" was more-or-less the usual sentiment). In time, Mom came to be viewed by people as almost a widow -- someone, that is, far more deserving of sympathy than of ostracism. Gradually, the role of victim at the hands of my totally narcissistic father was the one she chose to embrace.

At the bank, there was an initial vacuum left by my father's departure. For some time, I had been assisting him, so I was able to bridge some -- but not all -- of his duties. I was uncertain how everyone was going to react to my continued presence there -- if I even *had* a position, in fact: my father had more or less just carved out one for me while he was there, due to his influence. Now that he was gone, my status was tentative at best. There was some initial sounding-out of me on their part as to what my intentions were. But, I've always been a different sort than my dad, and once I reassured them that I had no intention of carrying on in the same guise as my father, they seemed to relax. I even recall saying to them, as they assembled to sort through the transition, that I neither condoned nor excused my father's behavior; that I assumed nothing at all about my continuing as an employee; and, that I was at their mercy. However, if they would still have me, I would be pleased to continue to serve in whatever capacity they deemed fit.

For a few days, I was on pins and needles as they conferred amongst themselves, as well as with the home office, as to what arrangements could be made about me. Truth be told, I was not even certain what I wanted the outcome to be myself -- whether it would be better to sever all ties with the bank and leave town (I had long been on the verge of trying to make this decision anyway); or, whether the bird in the hand of a stable position was more to be desired. When the decision came through to continue my position on a trial basis, I breathed a sigh of relief (though relief was far from what I was feeling).

For a long time, I'd been aware that I was attracted to men, and I would often steal away to the gay bar in Springfield to meet people and relax -- at least a little bit -- into the new skin I was trying out. The ability to actually live my life as a gay man in a town like Thornton was the thing I'd been wrestling with for a number of years now, and I was not optimistic about the prospects. The general support my mom and I were receiving was predicated upon sympathy. Were I to come out as gay, I had no illusions about how well *that* additional little tidbit would be received. Thornton was comprised mostly of farmers and small businessmen, located in the heart of the conservative Midwest. Most of its citizens still went to church, and -- presumably -- considered being gay not only foreign, but immoral as well. I had no real basis for testing this, but, growing up with a presumption of heterosexuality had given me a pretty clear indication the town was not overwhelmingly inclined to embrace an "alternative" lifestyle. So, what to do? I could continue to run to Springfield on the weekends, meet men occasionally; but, if anything long-term were to come my way in terms of a relationship, what then? Then again, since that hadn't exactly happened yet, why worry about it?

———•———

The first time I ever ran into someone I knew at the gay bar in Springfield, I thought he was going to have a heart attack. I'd been coming to the bar for a while now, and had more or less gotten used to being there, more or less accepting of myself as a gay person. I'd met a few guys -- even gone home with one or two of them -- though none of those experiences had ever extended beyond just the one time. Still, I remember how nervous *I'd* been the first time I ever walked into the place: as paralyzed as a cat in a strange house, afraid to move, afraid even to look around at anyone or anything. I recognized Ben from a number of years ago, when we'd been in school together. Sometime in high school, his father had died, and he'd moved outside of town to take care of his mom, so I hadn't really seen him in a few years. But, I knew him, all right. I watched him for a moment at the bar that night, seeing how scared he was to talk to anyone. Remembering how nervous I'd been *my* first time, I moved up to him slowly and -- as low-key as I could -- said: "Hey, Ben. How you doing?"

The look on Ben's face was as shocked and mortified as anything I've ever seen: not only to be at a gay bar for presumably the first time in his life, but also, to be recognized by someone he knew while he was there.

"Hey, Greg," he said, his face an absolute mask of terror. "Wow, small world, huh? Long time no see."

He was striving for a note of levity, but I knew he was panicking inside, the way I would have been not that long ago.

"Relax, Ben. It's okay," I said. Still, I knew no amount of reassurance from me was likely going to stop his freaking out. He just needed some time to get used to this new concept of himself, to adjust to it the way I'd had to, before he ran away, screaming, from it and its suddenly very real consequences.

"Oh, I know," said Ben, still struggling mightily to come to grips with the whole situation. "I'm just having a quick drink before I hook up with some friends who live in town. I've never been here before, have you?"

I had to smile at this: the transparent attempt to downplay his presence in such an establishment. "A few times," I said, trying to minimize the implications of that statement myself. "Can I get you something to drink?"

"Oh, no," said Ben nervously. "I was really just about to leave. I should probably be on my way. I don't want to keep my friends waiting."

"Ben," I said, as calmly as I could. "It's all right. I'm just asking if you'd like something to drink. I don't mean anything by it. You're safe here."

The look Ben fixed upon me then is one I'll never forget: full of such a scared intensity, vulnerability, and desperate helplessness that, if I had even the slightest doubt about his motives before, he completely and utterly dispelled them. It also made me, much to my surprise, want to take this flailing, fluttering, little creature and hold him in my arms -- a feeling I had never consciously had about Ben before, but which, too, was destined to be thwarted; because, like those wounded creatures we so often want to try to help, Ben panicked, made his desperate excuses, and then, I watched him as he almost literally ran away.

I'd lost track of Ben in high school though, as I said, we'd gone through grade school and junior high with one another, and he was always somewhere on the edge of my awareness. He was a tall kid, thin but strong, as most farm kids are. He had black hair, green eyes, and a kind of bemused look on his face always, as if what someone had just told him had totally shocked him. As a kid, he'd been kind of plain. In fact, I remember one time, in fifth or sixth grade, he showed me some warts he was trying to get rid of, and I guess that image of him kind of always stuck with me. Over time, he'd grown up, of course, but my image of him hadn't really changed from the one of that plain, surprised-looking kid with warts on his hand.

What struck me upon seeing him at the bar that night, however, was how strikingly handsome he'd suddenly become. In the intervening years, the features that had once been ordinary had somehow deepened and formed into really arresting depths and angles. Ben now had a face that -- without too much of a stretch -- could have graced the cover of a men's fashion magazine. Indeed, it was a bit astonishing how good-looking he'd become. I kept thinking about this after our meeting at the bar. Indeed, I'd never really thought about Ben that much over the years, but now it seemed I couldn't *stop* thinking about him. I kept seeing that scared, vulnerable look on his face and, more and more, I found myself wanting to sweep him up in my arms.

I kept thinking, too, about one particular time when I *had* noticed him hanging around the square in high school. He'd been out with a group of other kids, and I guess he was nominally going out with Cassie Hendricks though -- now that I think about it -- his heart didn't seem to be in it any more than mine had been when I was dating Kevin Treadle's sister. In retrospect, I was merely seeing her because I had a crush on Kevin. At the time, I suppose I thought it should look like I was dating *someone,* though Kevin's sister had caught onto my lack of enthusiasm long before I had owned up to myself any real responsibility for what I was feeling -- or, *not* feeling, as the case may be. The time I saw Ben out with Cassie, they were all just idling around the red-bricked square, the way everybody did on weekends. Cassie, the girl Ben was with, was a large-boned, crass girl -- one of those who likes to act tough to impress the boys, but who usually winds up just pushing herself further away from them. She was leaning against the hood of a 1978 yellow-and-black LeMans (my dad would, indeed, be proud of me for knowing that detail about the car) and was engaged in ribbing Rod McLemore about his girlfriend. Someone said something about her being flat-chested, and Cassie -- trying to curry favor with them -- said: "Shit, Billy Ford always says, 'More than a mouthful's a waste anyway.'" I still remember how Ben looked when Cassie said that: not particularly ashamed or judgmental, just uncomfortable. Anyway, I've always remembered that moment -- probably because I, too, could identify with Ben's discomfort, even though, at the time, I really didn't have a sense of what that discomfort was all about.

Thinking about that night at the bar in Springfield, flashing back to that look on Ben's face, I kept toying with the idea of calling him up; but, I was very focused on the thought of not spooking him. My sense of Ben right now was that he was like a dog who's been abused by someone; anytime anyone came around, his first thought was not of salvation, but instead of fear and escape.

I wasn't exactly sure where Ben even lived anymore -- just that it was some-where a few miles out of town. So, one day, on a Saturday, I decided to take a drive out past the furthest reaches of the town limits. It was a warm day in June, and the corn was already looking good, the leaves broad, flat, and hunter green in the sunlight against the robin's egg blue of the sky. A few, white clouds drift-ed slowly about; here and there, you could see the shadow of the clouds passing over the fields, or feel the thickness of the humidity. The day had the kind of laziness that days in the summer have, when things seem to be slowing down and filling up, the leaves on the trees expanding into larger, fuller versions of themselves. In a way, it was kind of like that with me, too: when my father left, there was this void where he'd always been -- more of a blackened crater, really. He'd always been one of those people who use up all the oxygen in the room; when he left, it was like I could finally breathe. More than that, though, there was space now to grow into without him around. I'd been working on filling the vacancy at the bank after he left -- not that I ever wanted to fill his shoes in any way. Indeed, my dad was like one of those prize hogs that rolls over on its young and suffocates them, and I never had any intention of trying to mimic or assume his over-sized proportions. My mom and I had definitely been squashed around him; but, with him gone, I was beginning to feel myself grow and fill out in other directions, especially when it came to figuring out who I was, who I wanted to be, and learning to accept my sexuality. It had been a struggle for me to get to where I was in terms of it. But, I felt like I'd seen some good examples of strong, proud, gay people, and I didn't see why I couldn't be one of them as well, at least someday.

When I got close to Ben's house (or, what I thought was Ben's house), I saw a faded, grey, two-story, Gothic structure with a white front porch held up by two square columns. The porch was just about wide enough for two chairs, side-by-side, underneath the somewhat saggy overhang. It wasn't a prosperous house or a poor one, just one that looked comfortable and lived-in. I slowed down near the fence, uncertain whether to stop or not, when I noticed Ben walking around out by the barn. He didn't know anyone was watching him and, as he stood there, it was like I'd just caught him listening for a sound from far away across the fields -- as if he'd heard something and had slowed down, trying to identify what it was, and focusing on where, exactly, the sound had originated. It was another private, unguarded moment and -- again -- I was reminded of how vulnerable he'd looked that night at the bar.

Before I could decide whether to intrude upon it or not, he became aware of my car and started, trying to see me through the slightly tinted glass. A bit flustered myself at being caught watching him, I rolled my window down and waved, saying, "Hey, Ben. It's Greg." I could tell he'd identified me a second before I said my name, and I was trying to get a sense of what the split-second look on his face might mean: was he scared I'd sought him out? Annoyed? I couldn't tell but, in a moment, he leaned forward slightly, loping into a resigned-seeming walk, approached the car and, for a moment, we just stood looking at each other.

"Hey, man," I said, finally: "I didn't mean to piss you off or anything. I just thought I'd see how you were doing."

"I'm okay," he said tersely, looking suddenly back across his shoulders, as if he'd heard the distant sound again.

"Sorry about freaking you out the other night at the bar. I just want you to know, I'd never say anything about that to anyone."

"No. I know. It's okay," he said after a minute, looking down as if undergoing a sudden change of heart. He looked at the ground for what seemed like a long while, then said: "You go to that bar a lot?"

It took me a moment to answer, too; but, finally, I said: "Not a lot. But, enough."

He seemed to weigh this in the balance, so I felt confident enough to say at last: "So, what do you think, Ben? You maybe feel like heading up to Springfield for a drink?"

In the car on the ride up, Ben filled me in on where he was in his life. His father had had a series of heart attacks while Ben was in high school, and had finally passed away two years ago. Ben's mother, whom he'd been taking care of since then, had a hard time coping, and Ben had to assume his father's role at the farm. His mother wasn't a big help with the finances or other matters, either, so Ben was really responsible for everything. Needless to say, this had really thrown a wrench into his plans and, talking about his father, he choked up in a way that made me envious: I'd never felt that way about *my* dad. It also made me understand that, not only was the grief still raw, but there was a lot of pent-up frustration about his current lot, too. I commiserated as much as I could, telling him what he didn't know about my own father's departure from town, and the way I'd felt about it.

When we got to the bar, I was a bit nervous Ben would panic again, the way he had before. This time, though, it seemed Ben was past the initial fear, though he did hang pretty close to me as we took a stool and had one drink, then another. I kept looking at him in the amber-colored light of the bar and, though I was trying to focus on his story, part of me just kept thinking: *God: I really can't believe how good-looking you've become!* I didn't say this to him, of course, though I'm not sure why: sometimes I think we want to run away from our feelings, even when the intensity should tell us there's something that really can't -- or shouldn't -- be ignored. But, it's like he, too, had suddenly grown into something totally unexpected, only he hadn't yet embraced this new version of himself, and probably had no idea how attractive he'd actually become.

Anyway, I just sat there thinking over and over again how good-looking he was, and after a while, I was barely paying attention to what he was saying anymore. Ben was still trying to make nervous small talk of some kind to stave off the forces telling him he was doing something wrong by being there, when suddenly I put my drink down on the bar, took him in my arms and kissed him. I can't even articulate what that kiss was like: how everything just suddenly felt electric; how it felt like the world was slowing down and somehow, now, for the first time, I was connected to it; as if -- after all the years of fruitless searching -- I finally had a sense of what it was that I'd been running toward.

After I finally let him go and looked at him, he looked back at me with such a bewildered-yet-grateful look, it was as though, all his life, that look of surprise and bewilderment he'd always worn had just been waiting for this moment when the two of us met and finally did what we'd just done. Leaning in, I kissed him again and, before I knew it, we were out the door and looking for somewhere -- anywhere -- to do what it felt like we'd been wanting our whole lives to do.

Quickly, we checked into a hotel just a few blocks away in downtown Springfield. I was bound and determined not to go to someplace sleazy like the Bella Vista Hotel, which had been the scene of my father's crime during the days of his dalliances with Gwen, so we checked into the Hilton: a tall, spindly structure know heareabouts as "The Prick on the Prairie."

The lovemaking was intense and unbelievable. What can you say about something like that? That every part of me seemed to fit perfectly into every part of him? That, together, I felt complete in a way I never had in my entire life up to that point? When it's right, I think you just know it.

After two, then three more sessions, glorying in the feel of each other and laying there in each other's arms, just soaking up the sensation, I finally got up and went to the window to look out. Below, the long, summer day was deepening into dusk at last and, looking at the scene, I was startled to see the little, red-brick streets and simple wooden houses of the Lincoln Settlement in town.

"Wow, check this out!" I said to Ben. "You can see all the Lincoln stuff down there."

Joining me, naked, in the window, Ben came up behind me and said: "Cool! I didn't know you'd be able to see that from up here."

I turned around to kiss him, marveling at the beauty of his body, and at the fact that here were two men, standing naked in a window as lovers.

"What would old Abe have thought," I said, "if someone had told him, a hundred fifty-odd years after he lived there in that wooden house, that there'd be a skyscraper next to his old neighborhood, and people would be staring down from the sky at where he used to live?"

"I suspect he'd have been pretty amazed," said Ben, shyly. "About as amazed as I am to find myself with you -- or anyone -- here, now."

We stood and watched the shadows lengthening and deepening around Springfield, then knew we had to get back to Thornton before it got too late: chores had to be done; Ben's mom had to be looked after; and, much as we'd reveled in this little interlude, our lives -- at least at the moment -- were back in Thornton.

Looking to prolong the inevitable, when we were just about back in town, I took a last-minute detour and drove around the campus of the local school, Thornton College. There was a perimeter road I sometimes took that skirted the campus in a big loop, winding up at the library. I'd pondered enrolling here many times over the years, especially now that my father was no longer around to prevent me from taking control of my life.

It was a beautiful night, the campus -- which was small anyway -- was really sparsely populated (most of the students were probably up at the bars around the square), so I parked the car in the parking lot behind the library, which had a roof shaped vaguely like a Pizza Hut, and we just sat for a moment.

"Why are we here?" asked Ben, at last.

"I don't know," I said. "I come here sometimes just to think. I've even thought about taking classes here. In fact, I just might go ahead and do it, come fall."

"Yeah?" said Ben. "I've thought about it, too. I was even all set to do it until…" Ben looked stricken and, again, I realized how much his father's death had affected him. One big thing we both had in common: we were both orphans of our fathers -- both left holding the bag -- just in different ways.

"Ben," I said, reaching out to touch his arm. "Things will get better. It's not always going to be so hard."

He acknowledged my touch for a moment, then got out of the car and started to walk, as if ashamed of the tears that were about to come.

I sat a moment, watching him walk away, then opened up my door and followed him. He'd slipped into a dark patch behind the library, however, and I'd lost sight of him. Afraid, suddenly, that he was going to run away again, I began to panic as I tried to locate him in the darkness beneath the stars, but I couldn't seem to find him; all I could see was the dimness of the stacks of the books inside the huge, plate glass windows of the now-closed library -- a world I still felt outside of, but very much wanted to belong to. After a minute or two of wildly casting about, fearing he really *had* run away from me again, I became aware of a noise over my head, and realized he must have climbed up a ladder of some kind, and was looking down on me from the hip of the oddly-shaped roof.

"What the hell are you doing up there?" I said, secretly delighted that I hadn't lost him after all.

"Nothing. Just hanging around. Come on up. It's a gorgeous night."

Reluctantly, I followed him up a thin, silver ladder onto the roof and, once up top, stood looking at the stars winking down on us from a black, indifferent sky. Suddenly, the world didn't seem so scary or antagonistic to me: it just seemed like it was *there*; like -- for once -- it was slowing down enough for me to be able to catch up to it. Ben was sitting near the edge, and I came over to join him. I can't even tell you how right and natural it felt to sit down beside him then -- sitting, instead of chasing. *Maybe*, I thought suddenly, *all the years of running away, all the issues of abandonment by my father, by Ben's, had led us here to finally discover ourselves -- to discover each other. Maybe our fathers both had to leave in order for this to happen at last.* I had no idea how the town would react if it got around about us. But, I did sense that Ben was feeling something for me as well -- that something was on the verge of changing for us both.

I wanted to say so much, but I was afraid to. I wanted to say: "Ben, I'm tired of not being honest about what I feel. I'm looking for someone I can trust, someone I can stay with, and who'll stay with me. I'm thinking maybe there's a chance that person might be *you*."

But, I didn't wind up needing to say anything because, at that very moment, Ben leaned his head against my shoulder and, looking out into the darkness across the campus and the town, it was exactly like it had been in the hotel, gazing down from above at Lincoln's little neighborhood: that same sense of everything seeming small and different now: changed. I didn't know if Ben and I would work out; or, even if we *did* become a couple, whether we'd be able to stay in a place as small as Thornton. I only knew one thing for certain as we sat there locked in each other's arms: I was never going to run away from something as good as *this*.

THE VOICES

———

STEVE NORBERG STOOD IN THE harsh, fluorescent glare of his dorm room mirror, trying to decide whether he was really going to apply the mascara he had purchased that afternoon at Pamida, the local thrift store chain in Thornton. An inner voice was telling him this was a small town, a small campus, and he should exercise some caution; yet, this was the same voice he had always listened to, and he was tired of being its slave.

Steve lifted the small, curvy eyelash brush out of its long, slim tube and brushed the glossy, black liquid on his lashes carefully. After finishing both eyes, he stood back and looked: the effect was not as pronounced as he'd expected, so he took out the eyeliner and began tentatively tracing a thin line over and under each eye. This time, the effect was much more noticeable, but still perhaps a bit too subtle. Steve had had a hard time deciding on a proper shade of eye shadow and, as he'd stood at Pamida, contemplating the multitude of choices running from chalk to charcoal, he could feel the eyes of passing housewives with their children bawling in shopping carts looking at him curiously. Finally, a saleslady asked him if he needed help, and he had said, as nonchalantly as he could, "I'm looking for some eye shadow."

"For your girlfriend?"

"No, for me."

"Okay," said the saleslady, who looked precisely like a stereotypical mother, and whose dark brown hair was permed and dyed so precisely it might have been a wig. "Well, what color were you thinking of?"

"Which one's the most popular?"

"Blue, I suppose."

"And which one's least popular?"

"*Least* popular?" said the woman, taken aback. "I don't know. Maybe black?"

"Then, give me that," said Steve. "Because that's what I'm going to be."

———◆———

Steve had come to Thornton College intending to make a splash. The school was small -- fewer than 500 students -- and, in many respects, exactly the wrong kind of place for someone just beginning to assert that he was gay. In Steve's high school, which had been many times larger than this entire college, the temptation to bury himself -- never to attract any attention to himself and his seemingly illicit desires -- had been overwhelming. He could still recall vividly nearly every instance in which he'd denied himself and who he wanted to be -- times when he'd had a sudden urge to pierce his ear and start wearing an earring to school, but squelched it; or, an urge to buy a pink shirt, only to chicken out in fear of being called a sissy. In a very real sense, the anonymity of a large state school would have been perfect for him to be able to disappear into the crowd but, after years of listening to the threats and bullying voices of the rural kids in his hometown, and the idle, odd, negative comments from his evangelical Christian parents about the "gay lifestyle," he was sick of toadying to the ignorance of such people. Only in a setting as small as Thornton did Steve feel there would be no going back on who he was; and this was, essentially, why he had chosen to come here: he was giving himself an ultimatum.

As Steve finished putting on the lipstick (a not-too-outrageous but, nevertheless, unmistakable, shade of red), Steve's roommate, Bill, came in. Bill was a computer nerd: he actually wore a calculator strapped to his belt, and plaid, button-down shirts with plastic pocket protectors for his pencils.

"Jesus," said Bill. "What are you doing? You look like a fag."

"Harsh, but accurate," said Steve, who had wondered how his being gay was going to go down with his roommate.

"What do you mean? You mean you *are* gay?"

"You're very quick," said Steve, steeling himself to be purposeful as he picked up the heavy, black eye shadow and began to apply it. The effect was somewhat ghoulish, like Gloria Swanson at Halloween, but he had gone this far, and so he continued applying.

Bill watched him a moment, still incredulous. "You're not going to wear that shit to dinner, are you?"

"Why else do you think I'm putting it on?"

Bill stared at him. Then, he said purposefully: "You try any shit with me and I'll pound your ass."

It was odd, thought Steve, how even the nerdiest of boys, when threatened, could suddenly become almost fearsome. "Don't worry. You're not my type," he said, already having prepared this particular response.

Steve had to congratulate himself on his nonchalance with Bill. Still, it was one thing to be flip with his roommate; it was quite another to walk across the close-cropped, yellowing lawns decked out like David Bowie, descend into a cafeteria full of central Illinois, corn-fed, blond-haired, blue-eyed kids, and attempt to act as though the look wasn't anything unusual. He'd been braced for people staring -- had been ready, even, for the threat of bodily harm; but, pulling off the kind of bored look that said, "Hey, this is no big deal, I wear makeup all the time," was beyond him, and he soon found himself cowering alone with his tray in the cafeteria, a look of mild defiance and despair turning his face into an almost literal mask as he endured the stares, the snickers, the imagined insults.

He almost missed it, then, when a heavy-set girl in a beige, chenille sweater stopped beside him and said, "Are you a Theater major?"

Looking at her more closely, Steve realized he had been mistaken: she was not heavy-set, just enormously well-endowed, with rounded shoulders, long, straight, black hair parted in the center, and a beatific look of contentment upon her face, as though she'd been inducted into some cult. "I beg your pardon?" said Steve.

"I was just wondering if you might be a Theater major."

"No," said Steve.

"Oh," said the girl. "Because *we* all are." She waved at a table full of friends, all wearing what looked like thrift-store clothing, accented by 'do-rags and assorted single earrings. "Would you like to join us?"

"Sure," said Steve, his impressions of her motives for asking undergoing a radical shift as he slid over.

"I'm Marci," said the well-endowed girl.

"Steve."

"Hey, great eye shadow," said a loud-mouthed girl with red hair sitting next to Marci. She was wearing heavy eye shadow herself, not very expertly or becomingly applied, so Steve wasn't exactly sure what to make of her compliment. She had on a poisonous yellow scarf that didn't match the red color of her hair at all. "I'm Ronda," said the girl. "You might as well join us. You're not going to find anyplace else to park yourself in this little freak show."

"Thanks," said Steve.

"So," said Marci. "Where are you from?"

"Up near Chicago," said Steve, who actually came from Peoria, but hated how Midwestern and clichéd the name of his hometown sounded.

"Do you always wear eye shadow?" asked Marci.

Steve sensed that she wasn't trying to make fun of him: she simply wanted to know; and, in the face of her surprising kindness, he found himself now confessing the truth. "Actually, no. I just wanted to try it, and so I did."

"We have to listen to these little voices sometimes," said Marci. "They're trying to tell us something -- something about ourselves, or what we're lacking."

Steve looked at her a moment, startled, and profoundly touched. "I agree. I think that's why I did it."

"I'm glad you did, " said Marci, smiling.

"We're in the distinct minority," said Ronda. "Look at all these carbon copies. God, it's like the Stepford campus around here."

"And what little voice made you choose Thornton?" continued Marci.

"A voice I probably should have ignored," said Steve.

"Nonsense," said Marci. "You're here for a reason. We just have to figure out what it is."

Shortly after this, Steve found himself sitting in the local college bar with Marci and her other friends one evening. Actually, he guessed they were *his* friends now as well, though he soon realized he had only a very limited interest in the theater, so his companions' endless chatter about Pinter, Pirandello, and Beckett had little or no interest for him. The bar itself was a hole: a gothic, Norman Bates-ish thing, full of a kind of decor that could only be described as Southern grotesque. Everything on the jukebox was 10 years old at least: songs like *Knights in White Satin*, or faded country hits, and the only people who ever came here were miners after the third shift (*Sixteen Tons* was playing at the moment), and under-age college students who couldn't get served anywhere else. Since there was nothing else to do in the town but drink, most of the students wound up at Frankie's sooner or later, though many of the students were fairly uptight, and the school itself had only eliminated mandatory chapel four years earlier. This was the kind of student body into which Steve had chosen to insert himself -- a choice he was beginning to have serious second thoughts about.

Sitting there variously in their Mexican serapes, capes, blue jeans with red suspenders, and bowler hats, he and his friends looked like refugees from a production of *Godspell*. Indeed, they looked like no one else in town. There were five of them that night: a gorgeous, faun-like man with black, curly hair and the gently sensitive nature of a gay man -- though, despite Steve's two drunken, late-night attempts to entice him into some sort of sexual exploration, he had proven maddeningly heterosexual; Marci, tonight wearing a cape, and whose enormous endowment might lead one to conclude she was loose, but who was, in fact, surprisingly inexperienced (she had an inordinate fondness for horses, Emily Dickinson, witches, and unicorns, and was -- despite all indications to the contrary -- apparently, still a virgin); loud-mouthed, red-haired Ronda, who was in love with the last man, a tow-haired, bleached-out, nastily funny gay man who both cultivated and, at the same time denied, his resemblance to Graham Chapman, the unapogetically gay member of the Monty Python crew.

While Steve liked having a group of friends to hang around with -- however tangential his association was -- the downside of tagging along with this crew, in particular, was that it seemingly meant exclusion from other little groups of friends he might have wanted to belong to, such as the one including Kyle Rhodes, his floor counselor, who was sitting at the other end of the bar with two other friends, totally oblivious to Steve and his group. Kyle was a tall, lean, dark-haired, athletic type, and ever since the first day Steve had seen him during orientation, then learned he was his floor counselor, he'd been absolutely consumed with attraction, awe, and hopelessness. Whenever he looked at Kyle, he felt something deep within him shift and gravitate.

Steve and his friends had been teasing each other about who was, or wasn't, sexually uptight; who was, or wasn't, sleeping with whom -- despite any real first-hand knowledge of what they were claiming as absolute gospel. Steve, who had abandoned his eye make-up in defeat for a while, had been glancing all evening longingly toward Kyle, who had his arm tantalizingly around the neck of another freshman whom Steve wouldn't have been at all surprised to find out was gay. Suddenly, Marc -- the tow-headed, Monty Python look-alike -- said mischievously, "Steve has the hots for Rhodes."

"I do not," said Steve, defensively.

"Ew," said Ronda. "That tool?"

"He does have kind of a cute butt," said Marc. "Still, Marci's right. He looks like the kind of guy who's going to be 'Employee of the Month' at an insurance company someday."

"Well, you can just shut up about it, because I assure you, I don't have the hots for him," lied Steve. "Please! He's not even my type."

"What the hell *is* your type?" said Jones (the faun), taking his eyes for a moment from Marci's bosom, which he had been staring at fixedly all night long.

"Besides you?" said Steve, looking pointedly at Jones.

"Isn't he your floor counselor?" said Jones, ignoring the remark, and looking at the handsome, boy-next-door features of the man two booths away.

"Yeah," said Steve.

"Oh! Oh! Mr. Counselor," said Marc, grabbing his crotch, "I've got a problem. Can you help me with it?"

The table laughed uproariously, and Ronda said, "I dare you to go up to him and say 'I love you.'"

"Fuck you," said Steve.

"Don't you wish," said Ronda.

"No, he wishes Rhodes would," said Marc, laughing idiotically, at which Kyle, Steve's floor counselor, glanced up at the bartender, then swung around and said:

"Hey, guys: you might want to keep it down a bit. Frankie's giving you the evil eye."

"Fuck Frankie," said Jones. "Fuck you, too."

Steve's counselor swung away from them curtly.

"Hey, Norberg," said Marc, grabbing his crotch again: "Keep it down, will ya?"

Everybody laughed once more, and then Jones said, "Let's get out of here. This place is a tomb."

They stood and started to grab coats, making their exit past the sober, dis-approving barman, and Steve looked at Marci, sitting calmly in the midst of the commotion in her cape like some oracular, Delphic priestess.

"Go talk to him," she said simply. "Love should never hide its face. It should always dare everything."

Steve hesitated, still uncertain, but Marc shoved him, and the rest of the group all ran away, looking back at their abandoned friend with malicious de-light. Marci gave him a final, sympathetic look, then joined the departing group as well.

Steve turned and glanced down the length of the bar. Kyle's face in the booth at the end was illuminated softly by the light, like a handsome doctor in a movie. Steve almost turned and walked out then, but stopped as he thought about what Marci had said. Slowly, he turned once more and began to make his way toward Kyle and his group.

That's when the terrible optimism began.

———

Of course, it had been a disaster, which was no surprise: Steve didn't really know any of the three of them and, in their eyes, he'd been part of a wild crowd that had been behaving badly in the bar. Still, after he'd made the effort to join them, he would have thought he might get a little bit of sympathy from Kyle, who *was* his floor counselor, after all.

Instead, even as he sat, he could practically see the hackles rising in them: here was this weird kid suddenly joining them, and why? For what reason was he pushing into their little group?

Kyle had quickly introduced him ("Guys, this is Steve. Steve's a freshmen on my floor"). Then, Kyle had introduced the friends sitting with him: Craig was a bearded, artsy-looking type. Like Kyle, he was a senior, and someone who wouldn't have been far out of place in the group of friends Steve had just abandoned. Kyle's other friend, Justin, was a freshman, too, and the instant Steve shook his hand, Steve felt a slight, defensive force field being thrown up between them, like the ones in an episode of *Star Trek*. There was a flicker of something like recognition in the look between them, too and, in a flash, Steve thought: *this guy's here because he's in love with Kyle, too!*

Indeed, things didn't get any better after that. In an effort, presumably, to lessen the awkwardness of their suddenly interrupted evening, Justin had asked Steve whether he was a theatre major, to which Steve had replied -- a bit melodramatically, granted: "Oh, God knows what I am. I'm kind of always in a perpetual state of identity crisis, so I guess the theater's as good a place for me as any." This sudden confession had made things even more awkward, as it appeared all of them were suddenly recollecting his earlier, mascara-wearing attempts, though he wasn't actually certain any of them had seen him in his glory. Still, it seemed to focus them all on the fact that they had very little in common. Stupidly, Steve had wound up practically insisting they all leave the bar and go back to the campus to party -- a thing Steve didn't want in the least, and which he'd only suggested because he found their scrutiny almost unbearable. They seemed to scream their disapproval of him with every terse word and reserved gesture; and, the whole time, he felt like a boat drifting further and further away from them -- from the dock he so desperately wanted to be tied against, which was Kyle. Feeling ever more helpless as the evening wore on and his ostracism deepened, he kept looking at the other freshman, Justin, curled up against Kyle in the booth like some favorite, adoring cat. Indeed, it galled him that -- even though he'd been trying to find his way in an admittedly outrageous manner -- at least *he* was being honest about the fact that he was different, not trying to project some sham of normalcy, like Justin.

As Steve thought about it the next day, a stubbornly bitter streak erupted in him at Kyle's inattention to him and, over the next few days, Steve made a point of joining Kyle and his friends uninvited at meals, tagging along with them to the library and the like, all the while encountering their evident frustration.

After a while, it actually began to give him a spiteful thrill to see how exasperated Justin would get whenever he appeared, and to watch Kyle squirming and struggling nobly against telling him simply to get lost. They were jerks, the three of them, his counselor maybe more than any of them.

But, whenever Steve saw how easily and naturally Justin had joined with them to create their own, clique-ish little triumvirate, he couldn't help feeling envious, and more than a bit burned. Every time he saw the three of them together, he had all he could do to stop himself from running across the quad screaming: "Justin's in love with you, Kyle, you idiot! Don't you see that? How blind can you be?" Still, he knew the reason the sight of the three of them together upset him so much was that he was in love with Kyle, too, but for a different -- perhaps more desperate and ridiculous -- reason: Kyle didn't care a whit. Indeed, Kyle had become a kind of obsession with him, precisely because he *was* so totally indifferent to him. It drove Steve crazy that, despite his attraction to Kyle, in particular -- and men, in general -- at least he was trying now to be honest and up front about it, while that other conniving little twerp, Justin, hid it and reaped the benefits of his continued deceit.

One day, as he was entering the dorm after class with his usual coterie, they spotted a fall-colored notice on the dormitory billboard announcing the upcoming Harvest Ball.

"You've got to be kidding me," said Jones. "They still have 'Harvest Balls' here?"

"They do," said Marc. "But it's not about harvesting your balls the way you mean."

"Ha, ha," said Jones.

"Oh! Wouldn't it be cool to crash the dance in, like, drag or something?" said Ronda, her hard, blue eyes flashing with malicious glee.

Given his present, contrary frame of mind, his sense of hopelessness about ever fitting into the student body here, and the seeming impossibility of ever making Kyle like him, something in Steve crystallized at this point, and he suddenly decided to make his estrangement final. Caught up in the enthusiasm of the moment, he heard himself saying: "Yeah! I could come in wearing, like, a studded leather collar." Even as he said it, though, he had no idea where in the world he was ever going to find one.

"And I could lead you all around the dance floor on a chain like a dog!" said Ronda.

"Yeah," said Steve, who felt a sudden stab of sadness at the mental picture this presented, but waved it off as he imagined the effect of trashing such a staid event.

The evening of the dance, however, he realized how badly he'd miscalculated. They did, indeed, wind up appearing as they'd described, Steve wearing a huge, black leather collar with large, silver studs (he'd borrowed it from Ronda who, of course, had one); Ronda dressed from head-to-toe in black leather, her black fishnet stockings in tatters and holding the other end of a huge silver chain as she led Steve around. The now-cleared dining hall was sparsely populated, its chairs shoved up against the wall, and the band installed in the space normally occupied by the salad bar. Appearing in such garb and being degraded in the guise of an s/m fantasy was not the hardest part or the miscalculation, however: the hardest part was the moment his eyes met Kyle's as he crawled around the dirty, hard, white-tiled floor and watched as the gulf between him and Kyle became fixed forever. At that moment, he realized that he was now, irrevocably and by his own choice, going to be viewed by everyone like some caged animal that needed to be kept behind a fence. But, even harder to swallow was that the person on the other side of the fence he most wanted to come pet him had no idea what a gentle, loving, and loyal creature he actually was.

One afternoon, as he was sitting in the curved, red-brick, 70s-era lobby of his dorm watching TV idly before his class, Steve saw Hugh Nordstrom walk in. Hugh was a senior, a huge, bodybuilder type whom Steve had actually seen his first day at Thornton. That day, Steve and all the other freshmen had been assembled in the upstairs lobby, listening distractedly to the dorm's Resident Advisor walk them through their orientation. As he watched, Hugh had emerged from the communal shower room adjacent to the lobby, dressed only in a towel. He could still recall the thrill of seeing Hugh -- quite possibly the best-built man he'd ever seen, with a chest that looked to be two feet thick; thighs like tree trunks; and arms with impossibly huge biceps -- bounce wetly down the hallway, seemingly oblivious to the group gathered behind him on the flattened, beer-stained, plaid chairs; oblivious, that is, to anything at all, save for his own physical perfection.

As Steve watched him in the lobby today, Hugh walked up behind a fellow member of the soccer squad, wrapped both his arms around him, and heaved him in the air. The fellow teammate -- large himself -- looked first annoyed, then terrified, to see that it was Hugh. Hugh toyed with him, dragging him first one way, then another, all the while not slacking his embrace a bit. Hugh made heavy, exaggerated, butt-fucking motions, and the man -- now mortified -- began to plead: "Hugh, cut it out. I give." Then, yelping finally: "*ALL RIGHT, HUGH! GOD DAMMIT, I GIVE!*"

Steve watched the man shake Hugh off, at last; and the man -- too embarrassed to look at anyone in the lobby -- turned to look at Hugh. Hugh's face was stony beyond a somewhat defiant look of victory and, suddenly, Steve recalled an odd fact he'd recently learned in his Animal Behavior class: that male polar bear will sometimes turn upon their own young and eat them. Steve also thought he saw, in Hugh's expression, the hurt look of an overgrown adolescent who's been reprimanded by his parents for not knowing his own strength. Also -- and this was what absolutely amazed and riveted him: for a second -- the slightest, briefest second -- there seemed to be almost a questioning look on Hugh's face; a scared, lost look, which Steve could identify with, that seemed almost to ask: *What would you think if I'd been serious about what I just did?*

The man began to stroll away, and Hugh, unwilling to concede that the interlude was over; or, perhaps, a little hurt and angry that his teammate had spurned him so brusquely, swatted him on the rear so hard his teammate nearly toppled over on the sofa. "Sweet ass," Hugh called out as he strolled victoriously away.

Steve watched in fascination as Hugh disappeared down the hall. He'd never seen anybody behave remotely like this before, and told himself that Hugh must have been kidding -- that he was reading far too much into it. Or, was he? Suddenly, outrageously, the thought occurred to him: *Was it possible Hugh might be gay?* He would never previously have dreamed it might be so, and yet... Also, much as he hated to admit it, given the brutal nature of it, the sight of Hugh's huge arms locked tightly around another man's body had given him an immediate erection.

Indeed, in the days that followed, this episode was all Steve could think about: that image of Hugh's power; of his arms wrapped tight around the other soccer player, massive and unshakeable; hips humping furiously; the insecure, questioning, almost vulnerable look on Hugh's face immediately afterward. As Steve imagined it, the scene gradually became an image of Hugh holding *him* in an embrace: Hugh's arms immensely strong, secure, enfolding and engulfing him. Was it possible, he wondered, if Hugh really *were* gay, that he might ever hold him in such a way?

The more he thought about it -- of that image of Hugh's enormous biceps curled around him, imprisoning him, the way they had the other soccer player -- the memory of it made him want to faint.

———•———

One evening, after walking back to his dorm, Steve opened up the doorway to his floor and felt a blast of noise and bong-sweet air assailing him. It was late -- past 10:00 -- but someone's stereo was blaring out the Talking Heads song *Psycho Killer.* Steve swore to himself, thinking testily that, if someone was having a party, it was going to be a long time before the dorm quieted down. Decisively, he grabbed a bottle of sleeping pills he'd purchased that day out at Pamida in preparation for just such an event, and swallowed the two white tablets. Then, thinking it would likely be a little while until the pills kicked in, he decided to take a shower. He'd been showering in the evenings lately to avoid contact with the rest of the floor; it just seemed simpler to avoid any issues that way.

Grabbing his gear, Steve walked down the hallway, its blue-and-white tile floor gummy with dirt and beer. Inside the bathroom, he placed his bag upon the metal shelf, and listlessly started brushing his teeth. He heard a sudden blast of volume down the hallway, then the door apparently closed again. When he looked up in the mirror next, Steve saw Hugh Nordstrom walking in behind him, towel tied loosely around his hips. Hugh's chest was covered with a fine, blond down, his shoulders looked like bowling balls, and the slabs of muscle in his back descended to a pair of buttocks huge as hams. Steve watched Hugh walk into the showers, a beer can in his hand, and noticed the glassy look in his eyes. Hugh was very high, and if he'd noticed Steve, he hadn't given any indication.

The entrance of Hugh threw an interesting light on things. He heard Hugh thrashing in the shower, whooping every now and then, and wondered what to do. Of late, he'd found himself fantasizing about Hugh, but he was also afraid of him. Yet, he couldn't help wondering if there was, perhaps, a chance that Hugh was gay, and was simply covering it up with a macho exterior. He remembered suddenly what Marci had said at the bar: that we had to listen to the little voices in our heads. He put his toothbrush away, picked up his gear, and slowly stepped into the changing room.

Inside, in the steam, he peeled his flannel bathrobe away, feeling frail and silly suddenly, as if he were a virgin readying himself for sacrifice. He hung his robe a little tentatively on a hook, thought again of Marci ("Love dares all things") and stepped into the mist.

At first, Hugh kept his back toward him. At first, the two of them together in the shower seemed no problem. Steve huddled in his corner by the door, Hugh diagonally across from him. Spray bounced wildly off Hugh, hitting Steve intermittently -- water that had once been on Hugh's body -- rolling past Steve's feet into the drain. Steve watched Hugh soaping up his massive limbs, scared to look too much, and yet, Hugh never seemed to finish: he'd been lathering his groin too long. As Steve looked now, he saw Hugh's knees were bent, his buttocks clenched, and suddenly he realized Hugh was masturbating. Steve stared, shocked, transfixed, but there was no mistaking it: the animal-like noises, the piston movements of his arm. Hugh threw his head back tensely, saw that Steve was watching him, and turned to face Steve head-on. Hugh's member was the thickest Steve had ever seen, still angry and erect, and, as Steve realized the effect it was having on his groin, he realized, too, that Hugh was looking at him coldly, staring through the spray.

There was a moment when Steve wasn't certain whether he should run or stay, a moment when the look on Hugh's face could have been threat or invitation. In that instant of misguided hope, Steve smiled nervously. Then, before he knew it, Hugh had grabbed him, shoved him to the floor, spreading both his both ass-cheeks, and thrusting an index finger deep inside him. Steve felt

Hugh fumbling at his ass, the huge, bald knob beginning to insert, then felt the burning, searing pain as Hugh shoved his swollen member deep inside him and began to pump. The pain was unbelievable. Steve was seeing nothing but white flashes behind his eyes, then a wave of blackness as he struggled for a grip upon the floor. He managed to brace himself at last against the raised ledge at the bottom of the door; but, with every thrust by Hugh, his head descended perilously close to smacking the dirty turquoise tile on the floor. Hugh continued pumping, shoving him with brutal force against the ledge. Steve's ass was numb, the heavy, wet-wool-scratchy weight of Hugh on top of him was crushing him, his folded leg in danger, seemingly, of snapping off. Steve tried to speak, to yell, but no sound came. Hugh's thrusts were growing faster now -- each lunge a blunted knife. Then, finally, Hugh finished, grunted heavily and shuddered, slapping Steve's ass so hard his head, at last, did crack against the tile. Steve felt as though his brain were bursting; he could see white stars behind his eyes, and merely lay there like a possum, hoping that, by playing dead, he would incur no further wrath.

Hugh pulled himself out of Steve's anus with a little plop, rinsed his member underneath the shower, then shook his head as slowly as a stallion. Looking down at Steve, he grabbed a yank of hair and pulled him back across the floor by it alone. Hugh's grip upon Steve's hair was merciless, the water like a blow upon his body.

"You tell anybody about this and I'll fucking kill you," Hugh said, snapping Steve's head forward as he let go of his hair. Hugh walked out to the bench, wrapped his towel nonchalantly around his waist, picked up his beer can, and was gone.

It was minutes till Steve moved, minutes as he lay there naked, water pummeling him, 'till the black veil lifted from his sight. He couldn't catch his breath, nor could he straighten up. At last, he lifted himself slowly, his bowels seemingly in danger of piling out onto the ground behind him. He shut the shower off and staggered out to sit down gingerly upon the bench; the pain in his rectum shot through him like a spike. His wet hair was dripping on his legs, his feet, but more than anything, he was afraid someone would walk into the room and ask him what had happened. Slowly, as the pain began to ebb, he pulled the towel down off its hook and dried his hair. More accurately, he just wiped the drips away shakily at first; then, when he had a little more control, he began to towel it, and sat back in the process, pain stabbing mercilessly again up through his anus.

Then, another thought hit. *What if Hugh came back?* Steve stood up gingerly, the blackness starting up again, and grabbed his robe. He tied the belt together swiftly, fighting the growing need to sit back down, then picked up his gear, and started down the hall.

Hugh's room was still as loud as it had been before, and Steve flew past it quickly, feeling frail and stupid, like a broomstick wrapped up in a trench coat. The noise from Hugh's room was so intense as he passed, he could feel the vibrations in the fabric of his robe.

As he entered his room and flipped on the bleak, fluorescent light, he paused a moment, nauseated and in pain. His roommate was not around, and the stillness and comparative quiet of the room assailed him like the abrupt step off the end of a moving walkway. He braced against the metal dresser, waiting for the wave of pain to pass, then glanced toward his unmade bed, realizing how much just climbing into it was going to hurt. He paused again, undecided, listening to the muted din from down the hall, thinking about everything that had just happened.

Then, suddenly, a kind of indignation started building deep within him. An insistent, little voice was asking him why he should run back to his room like this and cower like a rat? Another voice was countering that it was probably better just to forget it. Yet, the more he thought about it, the more he realized that *he'd* been violated, after all, not Hugh. So, what did he have to be ashamed of?

The more he mulled it over, the more he realized he simply wasn't going to run from confrontation anymore: he'd had enough, and wasn't going to take it any longer. Wasn't that the reason he had come to Thornton in the first place, to be a gay man, out and proud, and fuck the world and anybody else who didn't like it? Settling on a course of action now, he drew a pair of shorts on painfully, pulled his robe tight, and stepped back out into the hall.

His resolution wavered several more times as he walked back toward Hugh's door, but there at last, he took a breath and banged upon it loudly, so that he'd be heard. The Rolling Stones were blasting from behind the door and, after no response, heart thumping in his chest as if attempting to escape, he finally kicked and banged until, at last, the door flew open, and he saw Hugh -- shocked to see Steve standing there -- a weak, green desk light on in the background and several friends gathered around a bong, staring back at him.

"You forgot your kiss," said Steve, his voice drowned out in the wave of noise, though he was certain Hugh, at least, had heard it. He leaned toward Hugh, puckering, but Hugh shoved him so hard he crashed into the wall across the hall.

"Get out of here, you fucking faggot!" said Hugh, his face blanching in panic and surprise.

Hugh slammed the door behind him, and Steve stood for a moment, then started down the hall toward his room. He was probably a dead man now, he realized. Still, it gave him a wicked little thrill to see how panicked Hugh had been by his actions.

His smile faded quickly, though, as he realized the trouble he had likely made for himself, just as he always seemed hell-bent upon doing. *Maybe it wouldn't be so bad*, he tried to tell himself. *Hugh would say something to his friends like, "That little wimp was telling me to turn my stereo down."* Undoubtedly, his explanation would be something of that sort, and they'd believe him. Still, that wouldn't prevent Hugh from beating the shit out of him someday.

Steve entered his room again at last, conflicted, trying to resign himself to whatever might happen. Slowly, he crawled into bed, pain shooting through him with every agonizing movement. Settling in, finally, with a grimace, he glanced up at the light above, then swore: he'd forgotten to turn the room light off, and the thought of the stabs of pain he would have to endure by getting up out of bed again and turning it off made him feel exhausted.

Suddenly, there was a fumbling at the door and, for a fearful moment, Steve thought it was Hugh, coming to exact revenge. As the door opened, however, he saw it was his roommate, Bill, coming in with a pile of books beneath his arm.

"Oh, good," said Steve, warming to the sight of another person -- even his roommate -- in this instance. "I forgot to turn the light off."

"I'm not staying," said Bill, in the cold manner they'd settled upon with each other. "I'm heading over to the den to study. Gonna be a late night." Bill set his books down and exchanged them for another stack, never even glancing Steve's way, then exited, flipping off the room light as he left.

Fine, thought Steve, trying to reconcile himself to the repercussions of his actions toward the roommate he'd intentionally estranged, but feeling, suddenly, the weight of all the wrong choices he'd made already at this school, all the people he'd alienated: Bill, Kyle -- basically, the entire campus. He turned his face toward the wall, trying to cheer himself by thinking that maybe it wouldn't be that long until Bill came back -- that, maybe then he'd have a chance to talk to him, to try to bridge the gap at last. He lay there for what seemed like an eternity, but Bill did not return.

———◆———

In the morning, he awakened to the sound of voices. Bill was chatting to a friend, and they were moving noisily around the room, collecting books.

"Hey, it's after noon," said Bill. "Aren't you getting up today?"

Steve looked up through his haze, saw Bill with one of his friends -- a stocky, computer whiz who looked like one of those pudgy kids who pulled the wings off flies -- staring at him curiously. His rectum felt like it had been bored out, his eye was tender and, in a flash, he recalled everything that had happened to him last night

"I'm not feeling well," said Steve. "I think I'm just going to stay in bed today."

"Suit yourself," said Bill.

With that, they departed.

Steve lay for a while, blank-brained, too sore to move. Later, when the urge to urinate became so strong he knew he couldn't hold it anymore, he grabbed a plastic Thornton College cup from off his desk -- pain shooting through him as he reached out to retrieve it -- and carefully peed into it. After he'd finished, he looked at the acid yellow urine in the oversized white cup, embossed grandilo-quently in gold with the Thornton College logo. *Doesn't that just sort of say it all*, he thought: *this chalice of my beloved alma mater filled with my bilious pee.* He tucked the cup beneath the bed, worrying, as he did so, that he'd forget it, and wind up spilling it when he finally stood up. *Everything is such a mess!* he thought, the tears beginning.

Suddenly, out in the hall, he heard the voice of Kyle, his handsome, unattainable floor counselor, and hope sprung up within him like a mushroom from a stump. Maybe, he thought wildly, Kyle had heard what happened and was coming to comfort and counsel him! Maybe, finally, Kyle would pay attention to him, and would come and talk to him, the way he'd always hoped he would! Steve was on the verge of calling out, was pushing back the covers, moving to the door, despite the pain, to flag Kyle down.

But then, he heard the other voices in the hall and realized, with an equally negative jolt, that Kyle was out there with his other usual friends, Craig and Justin, joking on their way to somewhere fun. Standing just on the other side of the door from them, Steve hesitated, pain descending on him in a wave, clutching his dresser again. The bottle of Sominex he'd opened last night loomed before him like a vision in his nausea and pain. Steve would have liked some water, would have liked someone to come into the room and offer it to him, or place a hand upon his brow, nursing him tenderly, at last. Instead, he ripped the cap off shakily and choked more of the bitter, dry pills down.

The voices in the hallway rang out, mocking him. Then, they were gone.

THAT NIGHT

Hugh Nordstrom was not gay. But, that night, when he and Alex Bentley were sitting around in his room after working out, the windows open to the cool, May air, and their freshly pumped-up bodies cooling on the bald green sofa, Hugh had undeniably felt something. Alex had been sitting in his skimpy, cut-off shorts, his belly dimpled with its six-pack indentations. His chest was clear and unblemished, the skin around the nipples lightly ringed with hair, the pectorals taut and hard, and Hugh didn't know if it was the good buzz from the beer, the delicious, declining high from the power he'd felt in his body during the workout earlier that day, or the light glinting off Alex's beautifully wrought frame but, as the hour had grown late, Alex had jumped up to get them both one last beer, then flopped down shirtless beside him on the ratty sofa covered with its inadequate sheet, and all he knew was that Alex's head was suddenly pressed up against him, and it felt good. Alex stretched out with an exaggerated sigh, making himself at home, suddenly, with his head in Hugh's lap, smiling up at him cheekily, and the strange thing to Hugh was how *not* strange it felt. Hugh had leaned back, looking at his own newly pumped bicep, then looked down at Alex's naked chest. Alex's belly was flat and concave, the shorts stretched taut above his crotch from hipbone to hipbone, and it seemed so natural then to reach down and touch the chest -- this chest he had been so instrumental, after all, in developing into the fine hard mounds of muscle it now was. Hugh had cupped the nipple, and said, "Yeah, nice and fucking hard," as he gripped it. Still, in his mind, he had only been measuring Alex's progress: there was nothing at all sexual about it. But then, he had looked down at Alex's hair glinting in the light, with its little streaks of red and gold, and the next thing he knew, he was touching the hair, running his huge hand through it, fingering the nipples again, and suddenly, as he caressed the hard bumps of the belly, his hand was moving underneath the waistband of Alex's pants straight into the cave. Alex started, looking up at him strangely, but Hugh reached down to touch his face and, in a moment, they were both exploring each other's bodies with a sense of urgency and hunger that had led, eventually, to a hand job that was one of the most stimulating sexual experiences Hugh had ever had.

Hugh had never really been conscious of desire for Alex before this; nor was he aware of any feelings of attraction from Alex toward him. Certainly, they were constantly measuring and comparing each other's bodies when they worked out, but that's just what bodybuilders did, wasn't it? Since that night, neither of them had said a word about the finale of that evening, and it was almost as though it had never happened. Except that Hugh couldn't stop thinking about it. Had it simply been a momentary urge, an aberration? Had their hormones been raging to the point where they had merely taken care of one another, and that was that? It wasn't as though he was sitting around fantasizing about Alex; still, he couldn't stop recalling how it felt when he'd exploded in the tight pump of Alex's fist.

Hugh was a senior at Thornton College. Short, but powerfully built, he had always had a propensity for sports like football or weightlifting. He was on the soccer team here at Thornton, which wasn't exactly the right sport for him; and yet, he loved the cardiovascular workout it provided. If it didn't do enough for his upper body, it was tremendous for the legs, and he could -- and did -- always try to supplement the daily routines with three or four sessions per week of bench presses and other lifting workouts; Alex usually joined him on these. Alex was slighter than Hugh, with more of a lanky build. Alex was of Scottish descent, with reddish-gold hair, a long, lean torso which Hugh envied, and -- usually -- a day or two's stubble poking out around his lips. Hugh had noticed that, when cleaned up, Alex was sometimes strikingly handsome; but, beyond knowing that others found him good looking, he couldn't say his thoughts had ever ventured any further than that. Hugh himself was from German stock, with wheat-blond hair. He'd been blessed with a beefy, compact build: his thighs were 27 inches around, and completely solid. His chest was 54 inches, and his arms, when pumped, maxed out at 17-and-a-half inches. Hugh's newest addition was a mustache which, like the rest of him, was thicker than the norm. He thought it gave him a kind of rougish charm, especially since there was a darker undertone to it than the rest of his hair, which set off his mouth. Because he was so solid, leaner people like Alex fascinated him. Hugh was the kind who could have hoisted a refrigerator on his back without thinking anything of it; Alex, on the other hand, was taller, classier -- more like a tennis pro at some high-end country club. Much as Hugh gloried in the feeling of his own strength, secretly, he envied Alex's suave lankiness and elegance.

A few days after Hugh and Alex had relieved each other, Hugh had watched Alex in the dining hall, flirting with a girl he'd never seen before. Suddenly, Hugh felt strange, almost hurt. The two of them had seemed to acknowledge tacitly that nothing whatsoever was going to be said about what had happened. But now, as he watched Alex talking to the girl, the early afternoon sunlight shining through Alex's tousled hair, his almost Kool-Aid red lips hovering an inch or two away from the dark-haired girl's mouth, Hugh felt somehow betrayed. After what they'd done that night, he wondered how Alex could stand there so calmly talking to this girl: this moony, busty bimbo who had no idea what they'd done together. Hugh tried to calm himself. What did it mean anyway, Alex's talking to her? He knew Alex barely knew her. And yet, that fact hurt Hugh somehow even more. They'd been intimate with each other just a short time ago, and here was Alex -- his best bud -- talking to a girl he barely knew, instead of him. Again, Hugh tried to talk himself out of his response. Why should he care? It just meant Alex wasn't a fag, he guessed, and since he wasn't one either, what exactly was the problem? But, secretly, Hugh couldn't help wondering if they'd ever do what they had done again.

A moment later, Alex came back to the table, smirking.

"What's up?" said Hugh, affecting nonchalance.

"Not much."

"What'd that girl want?"

"Ah, nothing. We were just talking."

"How do you know her?"

"I don't, really. She's in my Psych class."

"Seems like she was flirting with you," said Hugh, thinking what he really wanted to say was, it seemed as though Alex was flirting with *her*.

"Oh, yeah, she's totally into me."

"Yeah?" said Hugh. He couldn't tell if Alex was mocking her, bragging, or trying to make him jealous. Any way he looked at it, he didn't like it.

That evening in the gym, though, it was just him and Alex again lifting weights, the way he liked it. As Hugh patiently spotted Alex, maxing out around 250 pounds on the bench tonight, he felt reassured, even as he felt Alex's focus wavering. Make no doubt about it, Alex was strong; but, where Hugh could bench press nearly 400 pounds, Alex always topped out at about 250 or 275. Hugh wasn't one of those people who sneered at people who weren't as strong as he was (few were). But, he did despise people who didn't take care of their own bodies. Alex struggled to bench the 250 tonight, then seemed to kind of give up.

"What's up, bud?" said Hugh. "Seems like you're not really into it."

"Nah, I'm just thinking about a test I've gotta take tomorrow, is all. I should probably knock off early and start studying for it, in fact."

"All right," said Hugh, disappointed. "Spot me for a minute before you go?"

"Sure," said Alex, who did, indeed, stand guard as Hugh hefted his enormous plates for a double set of ten reps. He almost needn't have bothered: Hugh had very little trouble with it. He'd wanted to push his limit tonight, but when he asked again if Alex was sure he had to go, Alex stayed firm.

Later, showering alone, Hugh felt unaccountably lonely, and decided to swing past Alex's room on his way back to his own.

When he knocked on Alex's door, however, Alex's roommate, Fred, answered, and said that Alex wasn't around -- that he hadn't been back there all evening, in fact. Thinking Alex might have gone to the library, Hugh headed across the campus to the vacant-seeming building, but Alex was nowhere to be seen there, either.

Next morning, still a little hurt and perplexed, Hugh caught up with Alex in the cafeteria, where he found him, once again, engaged in chatter with the same girl from the day before. This time, however, the two of them were sitting together, and looked -- if anything -- like the picture of two young lovers: they were cooing with each other, faces close, one of them whispering something to the other and then laughing as if everything were some huge joke.

"Hey, Alex," said Hugh, breaking up their little love-fest. "I looked for you last night. Where were you?"

"Oh, yeah," said Alex, looking suddenly stricken. "Marci and I had to do some studying for an exam."

"Were you at the library?" said Hugh. "I didn't see you."

"Oh, no," said Alex, looking even more uncomfortable. "The library was too full, so Marci and I just studied in her room."

"You should have dropped by afterwards," said Hugh. "You know I'm always up late."

"Yeah, I'll do that next time," said Alex.

As he walked away, Hugh had the distinct and unaccustomed sensation that he was being laughed at; that, as soon as he turned his back, Alex had turned to this new chick and said something like, "Christ, what's up his ass?" As he walked away feeling the humiliation and sick sense of inadequacy wriggle up his bones like weakness, Hugh had to ask himself, what in the world *was* his problem?

That evening, just before dinner, Hugh swung by Alex's room again. Again, Hugh had the sense that he was being a pest, and it was starting to make him mad. After all, hadn't he and Alex gotten together every other night? Didn't they always meet at least a few nights a week to work out together? Why should he now feel strange to be here appearing at Alex's door, just as he'd done so often in the past?

"Hey," said Alex, swinging open the door and plopping back on his bed as Hugh entered.

There was nothing at all unfriendly in what Alex said, and yet, Hugh sensed that something had, indeed, changed. "Hey," he said. "Are you ready to go grab some grub?"

"Sure," said Alex, although again, there seemed to be something a little guarded in his tone, something a little odd that Hugh had never heard before.

"Are we still on for working out tonight?" said Hugh, trying not to sound too hopeful, too invested in it.

"I don't know," said Alex, and there it was again: that guardedness, as if there *were* something he was ashamed of -- something he was trying to hide. Did Alex feel bad about what they'd done? Had he, too, been thinking about it?

"How come?"

"Well, I kind of told Marci I'd stop by and see her later tonight."

So, that was it: Alex was getting serious with that ridiculous piece of ass from class, and didn't want to tell him. "Can't you stop by and see her after we work out? I mean, I hate to break our rhythm. I think you can make 275 or even 300 by the end of the month if you keep on pushing."

"Yeah, well, the thing is," said Alex, almost bashfully now, "We're kind of going out to see a movie later. I told her I'd stop by and pick her up around 6:30."

"Oh, okay," said Hugh, feeling suddenly sick and deflated. He stood a moment, looking at Alex, his shirt tails untucked, chest bare, a little swatch of red hair running from his belly button down beneath the waistline of his brown corduroy pants. Thinking of the way he'd explored that area that night, he felt like a child who's just been told his best friend can't come out and play with him anymore. After another moment, still standing there awkwardly above the bed as Alex reclined in his beautiful, casual way, Hugh said, "Are you fucking her?"

"No, man, it's not like that," said Alex, suddenly not meeting his gaze.

"I mean, it's no big deal if you are."

"Yeah?" said Alex after a moment, looking up at him as if trying to gauge the truth of this.

"No, I mean, why *would* it be?" said Hugh, feeling very awkward. "I just didn't know you even knew her, is all."

"I don't, really. But, I think I might like to."

"Okay, that's cool," said Hugh, still feeling off-kilter.

"So, you're okay with it?"

Alex was looking at him almost fearfully now, and -- despite feeling exactly the opposite deep, down inside -- Hugh said, "Yeah, why not?"

"I don't know. I just thought…"

"You're not feeling bad about what happened the other night, are you?" said Hugh, trying to keep his voice level.

"No," said Alex, shifting to his side and drawing his knees beneath his chin, as if defensively.

As Hugh watched his discomfort, he said: "Because that was *nothing*. That was just two guys getting rid of an urge -- that's all."

"Yeah?" said Alex, hesitantly.

"Absolutely."

"Because I've been thinking: I don't want that to happen ever again."

"Hey, no problem," said Hugh, fighting to make himself still sound cheerful and disinterested. "I would hate to think something stupid like that would ever get in the way of our friendship."

Walking back to his empty dorm that night, trying not to think too hard about Alex and his girlfriend out on their date, and yet -- despite himself -- picturing Alex and that top-heavy bimbo slurping at each other's faces, he tried everything he could to make himself stop thinking about it. He'd never understood the attraction to girls like that: empty, stupid, soft.

Heading into his room, he cranked his stereo to the max with the Stones' *Beast of Burden*; listening impassively to that until Randy Potts, another member of the soccer team, popped his head in. Randy made a tooting gesture signifying, "Wanna get high?" to which Hugh shrugged. A moment later, Randy reappeared, looking badly in need of a shower, with his hair done up in a 'do-rag, his sweaty shorts gaping unflatteringly around his graceless, knobby knees, and bearing a six-pack and a little plastic baggie full of weed. He now had another soccer player with him, Bryan Hershaw, a tall, lean, New England type with a scrawny blond goatee and wire-rim glasses. As they hauled out the beer and started to pop one open for him, Hugh said, "Nah, fuck that. Let's get really wasted." He grabbed a bottle of Jack Daniels from its hiding place and took two gigantic swigs before offering it to the two of them. They took much smaller swigs, then lighted up a joint and started passing it around.

As the doobie came to him repeatedly, Hugh felt annoyed and restless. The drugs were having absolutely no effect on him, and so, he resorted again to huge, long, swigs of Jack to make him feel the buzz he wanted. The trouble was, as they sat there with their idiotic banter about the upcoming games, the drills, the coach, all Hugh could think about was Alex: that beautiful, trim torso hanging over Marci in bed -- those same, taut muscles he had helped develop in the gym, now being used for sex with someone else. Again and again, the image kept coming back to him: the perky moons of Alex's buttocks clenching and unclenching, muscles striating, hips delving, pumping, and thrusting. Hugh couldn't drive the image from his mind.

After an hour or so in the company of his moronic teammates -- both now totally wasted -- Hugh said at last, "Fuck this, I'm gonna go take a shower." He was pissed at the way things had gone with Alex; pissed about missing his work-out; about the minimal effect of all the alcohol and drugs; about the fact that now he had these cretins in his room and they wouldn't go away. As he stepped into the shower, Hugh caught a glimpse of himself in the mirrors over the sinks, and again felt proud of all the work he'd put into himself: he was a god, and Alex was an idiot if he wanted to waste his time with that stupid little slut.

Lathering himself in the water, feeling the cascading movement of the liquid on his muscles, Hugh flashed back to him and Alex grappling with each other that night. He could still feel the warm, hard mounds of Alex's pectorals, could still recall the strength, the hard virility, and yet the gentle care of their bodies yielding to each other as the thrill and the intensity had built. Aware he was erect now, Hugh reached down blearily and started pumping his organ, only too late realizing someone else was in the shower with him -- that scrawny kid, Steve or something, the one who'd worn the eye liner and dog collar to the school dance. As he turned around and saw the pitiful suggestiveness, the fearful, hungry look of wanting in the weak kid's eyes, it enraged him.

Suddenly, he grabbed the kid and then, before he knew it, he was pumping the scrawny kid's ass, that ass becoming Alex as he vented all his anger, hurt, and frustration. Now, as he climaxed hugely, body shuddering, Hugh grew aware of what he'd done and, in a momentary bout of fear, snatched the kid's head by his hair and choked out menacingly, "You tell anybody about this and I'll fucking kill you!"

Walking back, sick to his stomach, the smell of the weak kid's ass on his dick even though he'd tried to wash it off, it was as though he were a stranger in his skin. What had he just done? Why did everything seem totally confused, off-kilter, since that night with Alex? Was he supposed to think now he was gay, and that he suddenly loved Alex? What else would explain his inability to stop thinking about what happened between him and Alex that night, or his behavior just now with Steve? What in the world had induced him to beat that poor kid up, and leave him like that on the dirty, turquoise bathroom floor?

Returning to his room, Hugh was distressed to see the group of stoners had expanded. Coming in and sitting, shaken, on the same green sofa where he and Alex had been intimate together, he looked around and saw the glassy, blissed-out looks of all the others gathered in the room, and felt disgust. What were they doing to their bodies, all of them? What had he just done with his own? With Alex's? With that kid's?

A moment later, Hugh became aware of someone knocking on the door and, as he opened it, saw the scrawny freshman he had just raped, swaddled bonily in an ill-fitting robe and dripping in the doorway like some kind of witch. Hugh flinched, saw that the idiot was leaning in to kiss him and, with all his scared might, flung him mightily against the far wall.

"Fucking right!" said Randy blearily. "What did that faggot want?"

"Shut the fuck up!" said Hugh viciously, turning back into the room. He slammed the door and sat down on the sofa, as if he might faint. It was as though the huge muscles of his body were collapsing -- the muscles he had spent so much time building up, instead imploding, failing. He thought again about what he'd just done, about that night with Alex. Suddenly, he knew that no amount of bulking up or staving off with chemicals or alcohol was going to help him hoist this weight: this was a burden he had lost his grip on, and he feared now it was going to crush him.

A MOTORCYCLE RIDE

"Why must you cling to someone in order to live?"

E.L. DOCTOROW, *RAGTIME*

THE RECORD PLAYER WAS ON, spinning with a scarcely audible hum, and the needle was poised above the record halfway out as Justin came in: the cue was up. The room was lighted and warm as he moved further in, extracting a shudder that seemed to result as much from his surprise at finding it in visible use as from the unexpected warmth, and he stood disoriented for a moment. *like walking into a summer-empty house: the signs of life and people all around, but no one there. The same void Steve must feel -- must have been feeling: life and laughter all around, but no one there for him. Life's like a vacant dormitory: people either fill its rooms with love and memories, or they don't...*

He pulled the sweater over his head and made a vague, half-hearted movement toward the window. Punctuated here and there like exclamation points against the dark November sky, the yellow poplar trees bore witness to the presence of a chill, and he stared at them blankly for a moment. Then, he moved away, back toward the stereo, released the cue, and heard the music start.

A lyric melancholy filled the room: a timorous and deprecating sound, the needle carving out intensities in pitch vibration horizontally. *it didn't bleed.* Then, the room was silent for a moment as the needle fell into the space between two songs, riding in the grooves. So many separate lines: like a shock of chives -- tubed grasses -- smooth and cool, the fluids running just beneath the skin. Move vertically -- a skip against the grain -- and lay the grasses open. *just like then*, he thought: *Steve standing with the horizontal gashes on his wrists, red streaks descending from them on his upraised arms, imploring Kyle to hold him: Jesus Christ! He's slashed…*

His roommate swung the door wide, entering half-naked from the shower, fluffing up his hair. His unscarred wrist reached out to grab a towel and, as he did, the biceps moved beneath the skin perceptibly. *HIS towel, Kyle had said -- not mine. I will not use MY towel…* He watched his roommate carefully undo the knot around his waist and throw the wet towel, corded like a rope, upon his shoulder. *Let me see them! said the paramedic -- huge, authoritative -- kneeling down and trying to turn Steve's wrists. I can't help you if you won't show them to me. Stop fighting me! Let me see them…*

"Thought you went over to your friend's?" said his roommate.

"I did." *pull your hand out from behind your back, said the paramedic with brutal, practiced tenderness. You need to let me help you! Are you going to let me help you, Steve?*

"Aren't you doing anything tonight?"

WE are, WE are, they had said to Steve just hours before, the implication clear: we're not including YOU.

"Yes, Yes, I'm going back there now," he said, abruptly plunging past his startled roommate toward the door.

The air outside was cool, the moon high up, an icy white in carbon-paper black. He listened to the noises of the night, the breezes carrying the howl of nimbus raked across the tops of trees, the branches dark against the sky: a system of spasmodic tendons, and the clouds against the grain. He walked in silence, fearful, whimpering -- a stray, neglected animal: the runt who cowers near the ground and masturbates unceasingly; the meek one crapping in his pants beneath incendiary moons. *I'm just like him -- I've felt the same attraction. I've contemplated suicide as well. But, my God! To really do it! -- must have felt like drowning*

GET AN AMBULANCE!

And then, right at the end, before they took him off, Steve wanting Kyle to hold him, but he wouldn't do it! Why? That's what I want, too!

He felt the night breeze lick his face, dark waters beckoning with nullity and respite, like a vortex pulling to an everlasting blank, and dragging him through grasses moist as pubic hair. The scent of damp earth rose around him like an invitation to implant himself in its dank musk. Still, he continued through the fall-green lawns; on toward the arms of friendship, which he wanted to enfold him; on, on with nothing in the lobby of his mind except this fear, this strange compulsion, and the hoped-for warmth of love.

His knuckles rapped Craig's door, flopped back from unprotected wrists. *Steve Norberg slashed his wrists!* he wanted suddenly to scream, to fling himself into Craig's arms, *but that's what Steve had done -- had flung himself at Kyle, and look what had become of it.*

He stood and knocked again, but no one answered. *that's what Steve's whole life is like: him standing in the hallway, knocking on the door, and no one answering*

So, with no answer, Justin stepping back into the night, a ganglion -- that mass of nerves -- diffused intelligence; electric impotence; embarking on his separate path. He longed for love, for simple human touch, with all the complex chemical reactions following: a hand pressed up against another; arms to fill and, in return, be filled

"Hop on," Kyle said that night he couldn't stop remembering, Kyle's motorcycle luminescent in the moonlight.

"Really?" Justin said, still hesitant.

"Sure," said Kyle. "I'll take you for a ride."

and hopping on, no helmet, looking closely at the placement of his feet, so dangerously close to spinning wheels, and then not knowing how to ride: by holding on (and where? Put arms around Kyle's waist?); or, should he chance autonomy, be independent, self-assured and easy like his friend? They rode, and wind had swayed the bike and them, and he had ended up by clutching madly at the figure of his friend, as now, he longed to clutch at him again; because he couldn't be as independent as his friend, nor sway as easily as he, so clinging, though he merely wanted warmth, to hide his face in someone's breast and wane there, in the ease of an embrace

that's what Steve wanted, too, but never got it, driven to it, aiming for somebody's out-stretched arms; just like a toddler in a swimming pool, the father beckoning for him to jump: too many times, it seemed, the father missed the child

Exiting Craig's dorm, he saw the moon had left the sky and all that gave the darkness form were lights from other dormitory windows, scattered in the night, each kindling their square of space, the way a match flares out and lights the face of someone smoking in a bar. So they, too, beckoned with a warm familiarity; like singular, attentive beings; like a home. He picked out Kyle's small square of light -- like picking out a star to make a wish upon amidst the multiplicity of small lights in the universe -- and started walking toward it once more, quietly.

Then, he was knocking on the door and Kyle was opening it up.

"Just! Are you okay?"

"I'm not too sure."

"I know. Where's Craig?"

"I couldn't find him!" Justin blurted out.

"That's all right. We'll tell him everything tomorrow. It's been a rough night."

And he, now, hesitantly: "Steve got off to the hospital okay?"

"He seemed to be alright, considering. They'll probably keep him there a while."

And Justin struggling now with asking this -- the issue that was bothering him so much: "Kyle, just before Steve left, he asked if you would hug him, and you wouldn't do it."

"I know," said Kyle, looking stricken. "I almost did. But, in the end, I decided it might do more harm than good. It felt like I might be leading him on..."

"Sometimes, I've felt like him -- that desperate," he hastened to add.

"Me, too. We all need love."

"He just wanted somebody to hold him!"

"I know. But, I didn't feel like that somebody should be me."

I want somebody to hold me! he wanted suddenly to scream, to have Kyle hear there was no difference, he was the same as Steve: that poor, deluded, unreciprocated queer. *No, no, can't say that, now that Steve has gone and done this, made his desperation real, and I am falling, falling in that same, deep pool. Will no one rescue me?*

But, no words came; none needed to. For, in that moment, Kyle leaned in.

His embrace was like a lighted room.

THE ANCHOR

SEPTEMBER 24

THEY ARE STANDING, MAN AND woman, on the bridge in autumn: two figures anchoring the campus on a windswept afternoon. I sketch them in my notebook from a quiet spot beneath an oak tree not far away. They are an ordinary pair, perhaps even a little nondescript; and yet, they are all the more irritating for being so ordinary. Like an anchor, they remind me of the stable sea to which I should belong. They are a weight that drags me down.

It is one of those startling autumnal days that seems to come out of nowhere, appearing so sharp and clear and cold, it's like a razor blade pressed against your wrist. Once again, I partake of all this beauty alone. I can't help feeling the colors would seem somehow less painful, the sun less glaring, if I were sharing the moment with someone else, rather than sitting here alone with my notebook open, attempting to capture something I am not a part of.

It is difficult to write today -- difficult to overcome this heaviness that makes me want to sink into the ground beneath this tree and disappear.

OCTOBER 1

We were sitting at the bar that night -- that wonderfully strange, gothic bar with the stuffed crows looking down from amid the trophy deer heads, the tin roof, and the heavy, ornate, crème-colored lights -- and there was Steve sitting at the grey Formica table, looking forlorn. I could tell right away he was in love with Kyle, the Peer Group Counselor on his floor: he was gazing up at him with that moony, rapt expression that can only be first love. Kyle, of course, was paying absolutely no attention to him, and it just broke my heart to see Steve sitting there, wasting his time pining after someone who was so unworthy of him. Steve is such a beautiful and unusual spirit! He's a bit uncertain who he is (who among us isn't?) and, of course, the local cowpoke population in this town and at the college think he's a misfit. Steve needs to be someplace more tolerant, like Greenwich Village or San Francisco, where he can be the kind of person he really wants to be.

I'd met Steve through some of the other theater majors and art students who huddled together in this little nowhere town; but, even in that group, Steve was a misfit. I'm not sure where Steve belonged, but it certainly wasn't with them. Still, if that was what he wanted…

We were sitting there having fun, and Steve was alternating between being morose and overly animated: never a winning combination, as I know too well. Later, I went up to him and was on the verge of making some cutting remark about Kyle; but, when I saw the lovesick expression on his face, I just didn't have the heart. Instead, I said: "Go talk to him. Love should never hide its face. It should always dare everything." I'm not even quite certain why I said it, but it seemed to have an effect. I was worried about him as we left him there. Then again, what can you do? After all, nothing ventured, nothing gained…

Oct 7

I was doodling along in my Intro Psych class today when the boy I was sitting next to leaned over to see what I was doing. I was drawing a figure with a pentagonal head, and he professed to being very interested in my motivations for doing that. I, for my part, pretended not to notice how obvious he was being. In truth, I'm not sure why I played along, except he is kind of interesting. I kept looking at the way his biceps curled beneath his short sleeves, and the reddish-gold hair poking out from underneath his arms. I'm not really sure whether I'm attracted to, or repelled by, this, and yet I keep staring at him, class after class. I was amazed he noticed me, really. He's kind of a jock, and could have anyone; and yet, there's an underlying sweetness and bashfulness about him I relate to. He's got freckled, sallow skin, and will be popular someday when he finally grows into his body and his skin clears up. Right now, though, he's like a puppy trouncing around with extra skin and floppy feet.

At any rate, one thing led to another, and he looked at more of my drawings after class. He said his name was Alex, and asked me if I'd like to go get a coffee. Instead, we wound up going back to his room with the badly stained green carpet, the empty, greasy, pizza box tops, and wet rubber smell of sneakers underneath the bed. There, in this veritable Taj Mahal, we made love on his dirty bedsheets. He smelled like all boys smell: that curious, metallic mix of motor oil and smoke. He looked at me like a beery-eyed drunk afterwards and asked when he could see me again. Every time I think about it, I want to throw up.

———◆———

Random notes: This is the period when every figure I drew contained some sort of cephalic distortion: mine, Steve's, Alex's. That word, "cephalic," always makes me think of phalluses and penises. Of *his* penis. But it really means *head*. His penis head...

OCTOBER 8

I could not think at all again today. I keep thinking about what Alex and I did in his room, and can't help feeling nauseated. What a debauch. What a debauch of art, to use my drawings as a pretext for having sex! I keep seeing him motioning me over to the bed, and me, trying to make myself believe he was the answer to my prayers. We embraced each other then, but even as we did so, I kept thinking to myself that, if anyone had seen us, we would have looked like two figures in a tragedy.

OCTOBER 17

I had a startling conversation with a girl today. We were standing on the quad and it was bitterly cold, but she had on only a light, letterman's jacket and her cheerleading outfit. I had on a formless, heavy, wool cape with a hood that makes me look a bit like Little Red Riding Hood. The girl stood looking at the ground as I continued the discussion from the Intro to Religion class we had just left, about the morality of suicide. I'm not even sure why I was talking to her, but the class had been interesting, and we were walking out together. Anyway, I was prattling on about this and that, and she said, finally: "Look, I really don't want to continue this conversation anymore. I mean, I've never seriously even considered committing suicide."

I was incredulous, and stood looking at her for a moment. "Ever in your life?"

"Not really, no."

I was speechless. Here before me was someone who, aside from an occasional, "I wish I were dead" (said just after an embarrassing social situation, I'm sure), had never seriously thought of ending the pain -- someone for whom the notion was not only foreign and immoral, but who also couldn't fathom the thought of why anybody else would ever entertain the idea, either.

But, I am very used to the idea. I live with the thought every day, like getting up in the morning and seeing my reflection in the mirror: so many times it seems almost attractive...

I have decided not to see Alex again since acting out our little tragedy.

October 23

Yesterday, convinced that writing and drawing are what separate me from my fellow man, I sat atop a windswept log at the far edge of the campus and opened my folder to the wind. I saw my stories and my drawings tumble across the field, where they caught, ugly and inelegant, on fences, rocks, the bridge that crosses the campus.

As soon as I had done it, I felt bad, and ran gathering them up again; yet, some were lost, and now my secrets continue to roll around the quad for all to see. It was like scattering dandelion seeds to the wind: it felt great while I was doing it -- that sweet dispersal in the air.

Then, I was sad, because all I had left was the ugly and denuded stump I still held clenched inside my fist.

October 26

A blustery day. The wind blew through the bare, black tree limbs, scratching at the underbelly of the snow-grey clouds. Somehow the crispness of the air made me draw up even further into myself. Everywhere, the dead leaves whipped into a scorpion tail and stung out blindly at the sky. The ground was frozen yellow-white, I was bundled up and walking slowly, pensively, as my feet knocked through the frozen mounds of each tree's fallen world. How soft my bones pull, yearning toward that mouldering; how peaceful that dissemination, scattered to the winds forever.

Like my drawings, like my dreams…

October 28

My roommate is worried -- says I never join in what the floor is doing, or see anyone. I sat quietly on the bed tonight toying with the cover of *L'Etranger* as she questioned me in her well-meaning way. I was hoping to find some way to spare her those pains, but she was hell-bent upon cheering me up. At other times, her need to make me happy might have rankled, but tonight, I felt strangely acquiescent -- even needful -- as her brown eyes stared at me moistly in the semi-light. I felt almost attracted to her for a moment -- something I've felt from time-to-time with other women, but never as consciously nor as problematically as tonight, when my thoughts were already a twisted mobile.

Just as I was feeling it most, she moved, and I felt a little barrier spring up between us invisibly, though I'm not sure why. I only know that, despite the closeness I'd felt to her just a moment before, suddenly I realized I'd be no more comfortable unburdening myself to her than I would be emptying my suitcase in the middle of a bus depot.

October 31

Halloween: once again, I wear my ghastly mask. Tonight, however, I was mirrored by the pumpkin sentinels that lined the streets I walked: each garish grin ignited by the candle burning deep inside; the suffocating, thinned-out flame licking at the orange flesh inside and turning it to charcoal. Everywhere, the night was filled with darker concentrations, blacker holes: the children in their vampire outfits -- little bloodsuckers, as are all those who love or are *in* love -- moving furtively from porch to porch. What to make of all these random congregations in the night? The brief, masked meetings? The exchanges -- hungry hands -- until the hunger's momentarily sated?

I watch, distracted, in the street, as each group meets and moves on, wondering at the white stars mocking in their empty void of cold, black air above. Not far away, a white sheet floats and billows in a treetop wind, an earthbound ghost still struggling toward transcendence. In its brittle prison high above our heads, it snags and strains as, all around, the dry twigs clutch it in their thorny arms.

NOVEMBER 3

Today a girl -- Bryn, down the hall -- came by to talk about Camus. She's in my French class, and I've noticed her before. Still, I was a little surprised she came to see me. She came in and sat down and we chatted about the book. It was a little awkward for a while; then, we seemed to hit a good pace and things seemed more natural. I was becoming vaguely aware, however, that that there was something she wasn't saying. I could see it come into her face for a moment every time she looked away or at the floor. But then, she would completely dispel it with her next sentence. Despite my detachment in noticing that, I was interested in the discussion (I like the sense of alienation in the book), and I liked watching her as she clasped and unclasped her knees distractedly as she talked. There was something almost attractive in the way the whiskey-colored room light played about her light, brown hair.

Just then, I wasn't listening to her anymore, because I was conscious of the angle of her head, and of the lamp that cast a swatch of light obliquely toward her. Also, there was a tone beneath her words I was struggling hard to catch. I realized suddenly we were both observing each other, and I was trying desperately to decide whether she'd asked me something I was supposed to answer, when she said quite suddenly:

"You're so beautiful."

Taken wholly unaware, my first reaction was to laugh, but I perceived instantly that she was serious, and I stopped. "Well, that's a first," I said, stupidly.

"What, someone telling you you're beautiful?"

I nodded, feeling strangely constricted, and in unfamiliar territory.

"I find that hard to believe."

Again, I felt clueless as to what to do.

Then, Bryn said: "I saw your pieces in the student art show: they're excellent. I could never draw anything like that."

Inwardly, I cringed as I always do at what I consider gratuitous flattery, except that, as I looked up into her eyes, I saw an earnestness so bold and naked I had to look away. At that moment, too, I was remembering my pictures flying wildly about the quad, thinking: *Did I just throw all that away? Why did I do that?*

"Anyway, I just wanted to tell you I admire you for having talent and seeing things the way you do, and that you're a really beautiful soul. Because I'm not sure you know that."

She rose then, crossed the trapezoid of light and stooped in front of me a moment to give me an embarrassed little hug; then, she was gone.

I felt as though I were in an elevator that was having trouble matching up at any floor, and simply stared at the doorknob, thinking: *I should chase her down, run after her.*

But, I was anchored to the spot -- absolutely given weight and specificity by what she'd done. I couldn't move, and so remained there, stunned, upended, wondering: *Why? Why had she done that? Why had she dragged me back to earth like that?*

November 15

An "up" day. Something happens in the air on cloudless days: a special bouyancy and lightness that inspires my soul to be as boundless as the light-filled sky. I walked along today and let the light wash over me, watching as the brown squirrels scurried over the yellow grass. The scent of dying leaves was everywhere -- that earthy, dusty, dry-leaf smell. Today, all things seemed somehow right, precise. It was the kind of day a child has as he rolls about the leaves, carefree.

November 19

I can scarcely catch my breath: Steve tried to kill himself. The boy I counseled to follow his heart has followed it, and wound up crucifying himself upon the wall of Kyle's indifference. Why is love so pitiless and heartless? What was Steve trying to do: drain away all traces of his pain? Was he trying to release all the blood from his body, so that he could then float free of the earth?

I want to stand out in the middle of the quad. I want to scream and claw and beat the ground.

November 23

Steve is in the hospital now. I saw the drugged-out shell; I saw the drooling, hopeless leer. Oh, Steve! How could I have been so stupid as to tell you to follow your heart? How could I have ever thought it led anywhere but straight into pain?

Evening: Bryn came by to see how I was doing, but I couldn't talk: I'm walking novocaine.

December 1

Bryn came by to talk again today. At first I didn't want to, but she forced her way into the room against my opposition, sitting me down on the bed, and bringing up a chair across from me. She sat and looked at me a moment, then said: "I've lost my friend."

At first, I thought someone she knew, too, had tried to kill himself but, just before I spoke, she said,

"You don't even know that I mean you, do you?"

I was so startled, I didn't know what to say. "I'm sorry, I've just been feeling very upended lately," I stammered, lamely. "And then, you really took me off guard when you said what you said the other day."

"Did I?" she said.

Then, I don't really remember anything at all about what happened. I only know that when she came and sat beside me and put her lips serenely to my own, I felt my heart swell up so large I was really quite alarmed it might burst.

December 3

Two nights ago, I opened myself up completely to Bryn. It was as though I had lain myself out on the quad like my portfolio, and Bryn came and patiently picked up every page, reassembled them carefully, and paused to finger this or that image, and touch each little gesture and line. I never knew love could be so incredibly intimate, such a congruence of body-to-body, image-to-perception. It was as though I were no longer at a remove, drawing everything: instead, I was *in* the act, feeling everything for myself. In everything I've done so far, in terms of love, I realize I've been a complete bystander. This is the first time I really felt as though I'd come into my body, possessed each and every corner of it -- that I was suddenly *me*.

I realize now I should not have acted so rashly in opening my folder to the wind. This morning, as I walked across the wintry quad, I felt so curiously alive and springy that it felt like Easter. The quad was empty and blank, and there was no trace of any of my drawings anywhere. No matter: I've started some new sketches now, and hope to continue with more after finals are over.

I think, in spite of all, I was right in what I told Steve: love *does* dare everything if it's to be of any use. After all, where would I be if Bryn had not done so?

December 4

Talked well into the night with Bryn last night, and we made love again, hungrily, blissfully, gratefully. I feel as though we're on the verge of something exciting and new and scary, but scary in a good way. I told her all about Steve and what I'd said to him, and we talked about love and fear, and how love was like embracing something and letting it go at the same time. She berated me for being "like a rock" -- an immovable object for so long. She said she'd been trying and trying to push me, and had nearly given up in despair; I'm so glad she didn't. Afterwards, I stumbled back to my room, exhausted, and fell asleep like the dead.

The next thing I knew, my roommate was tapping me on the shoulder, saying to me in a patient, steady voice;

"You have an Intro-Psych final at nine o'clock."

I sat up groggily, swung out from under the covers, and stared for a good, long time at my feet upon the floor.

THE ROOMMATE

———————

*A*LL THESE YEARS I'VE ALWAYS *felt like You were there, Lord, that i could feel You behind everything, and now i'm not so sure, not sure at all. It's just, i still keep seeing Jenny lying on the pavement, the broken body of her lying there, the way Your broken body hangs upon the cross; but, seeing her there, the wounds were so real, the meat and fiber of her and the blood, i'm just not sure i did the right thing anymore and before i was so sure, i kept telling Jenny i was so sure and now i just don't know.*

That first day she and i met as roommates here at Thornton, i had a vibe even then that something wasn't right with her, like when i asked her if she was saved and she hesitated when she answered, that maybe i was there to save her someway, it just seemed there was something a little lost about her and i was so sure, and now i'm not at all, but then i was, and so i watched her day after day, talking to her about how the Lord was there to save her, and did she know that? From the way she answered each time, i could tell there was something wrong, that dismissive way, and when i kept at her, i finally even said, "Why do you always push me away when i ask you that? It's like you're trying to push the Lord away, too," and she said, "You don't even know. You don't even know what you're asking me." And when i said, "What? What do you mean?" Finally, she said: "I think I may not be right. I think there may really be something wrong with me." Then, when i pushed, that's when she said it: "I think maybe I do *need saving, but it can't be you who saves me." When i persisted, asking why, she said at last: "You can't be the one to save me, because I think I'm in love with you."*

As a child, growing up, i'd always been told the devil could assume many forms, that you had to watch out for him in whatever guise he may appear, but i have to admit, that one took me totally by surprise. Never in my life could i ever have imagined that right here, sleeping in bed next to me, night after night for weeks and weeks now, was someone who was harboring such unnatural feelings towards me, and right then, that's when i said it: "We have to get this demon out of you. I know you, and you're not a bad person, but we have to work very hard to cleanse you, because you can't be feeling these things for me. You're too good of a person to let the devil take up residence in you like that."

That's when i began to study, study really hard, about how you could cast Satan out of someone's body.

There was a lot of precedent for it, and i'd seen it done a few times in our church growing up. It was always really scary, you could really sense the power of Our Lord when it happened, the person always yelled and hollered when it was happening, it must have hurt a lot, ripping Satan out of your body when he didn't want to let go, but that's what really bothers me the most: Jenny didn't yell and holler when I was shouting scripture at her, she just started to sob, and finally she ran down the hallway and threw herself off the balcony and then she just lay there, broken, and it was like nothing at all had left her, except her spirit.

That's the thing i just can't get over. She wasn't protesting and yelling: she just looked unhappy, like i'd betrayed her and, suddenly, she just wanted to die -- to die and not be saved, and how could Our Lord of compassion and salvation allow a thing like that to occur? How could He just let Jenny lay all wounded and broken and not heal her like i believe, in the long run, He will?

And that look, that look on Jenny's face, like she was saying: "How could you do this to me, especially when I told you I _loved_ you?"

That's the thing i just keep seeing over and over -- that, and Jenny's broken bones, those bones i'd helped break, and that's when i get really angry, angry that the Lord, who's been my constant companion, who's been _my_ roommate over my whole entire life, how could He let something like this happen, and did i do wrong in what i did? i was trying to do what i thought was best for Jenny, but now i just think, more and more, what i did was wrong, and how could this be? i've always been brought up to believe the word of the Lord is infallible; that, "If you raise a child up in Jesus, there's no place else for them to go," but I'm beginning to feel more and more that's just not true.

i just keep thinking to myself: "How can this be right?" i've never, ever, doubted the word of the Lord before, but i just keep seeing Jenny's broken body and thinking: "This is not right, this is not right, what i did. How could Our Lord have wanted this -- to have Jenny lying there on the pavement three floors below, the life ebbing slowly out of her?" i just can't think Our

Lord would ever want that, but i've been told all my life that kind of thing is a sin, that it's the devil taking up residence in someone and all you have to do is drive the devil out; that, "Our God is a consuming fire"; that, "He makes his angels spirits, and His ministers a flaming fire," but now i can't help feeling in my bones it's just not right.

Then i get so mad i want to smash things. i want to rip the wooden cross from around my neck, the one i've always worn since the day i was saved, and now it seems i can't even stand the sight of it, can't stand the weight of it pressing in on me, so i ripped it off. But even that brought no relief: i still can see her body lying broken on the pavement, and then it's like i don't know what to do, can't find a place to hide, because i know in no uncertain terms that i did this, i'm the one who drove her down the hall and off that balcony, my certainty and my unshakeable belief -- my absolute conviction and my persecution of her, 'till she made this effort, which i now begin to realize was wrong.

And then i ask myself: "So, what's my penance? What is my atonement for my sin, for my inflexible belief?"

"Is not My word like as fire, saith the Lord?"

"Behold, the whirlwind of the Lord goeth forth, it shall fall upon the head of the wicked."

That's when it hits me what to do -- hits me so hard, so right, i don't even pause to ask myself if it is right or not, i know that it's the only thing to do: I'm going to cross the quad and turn his own fire back upon him, burn the chapel down and drive him from me with the certainty I had when i thought i was casting Satan out of Jenny.

i don't want him anywhere around me anymore -- don't trust him here beside me. He can go up in the flames and lie there just as still as Jenny did. i simply will not have him near me anymore. i'm going to drive him from my life once and forever now. i'm going to drive him out with fire, the way he made me drive my roommate off that balcony...

LIVIA, OR PARTIAL PARALYSIS

———

A STROKE IS WHAT THEY SAY is responsible: everything on the right side of my body is fine, but the left side is pretty much paralyzed. I get around okay using this cane, but it's the little things that get you, like this slight rise in the ground here. You probably didn't even notice it, but I have to walk completely around it because, as it turns out, you use both sides of your body for balance, and I just don't have any on the left anymore; hence, this small detour we're taking.

I hope you don't mind. I think, in life, you've to make do with whatever you've got.

When I first came here to Thornton, I couldn't get over how flat it was; now, I see every little bump in the way; there've been a number of them over the years.

Thornton has been a good place to live; but, being where it is, in the middle of Southern Illinois cornfields, it's not exactly a bastion of enlightenment. In fact, it's kind of like a monastery during the Middle Ages, seeking to preserve whatever culture it can against the vast, surrounding tides of indifference and even active antagonism. The college has always had a kind of uneasy position in the town. They call us "Thornies;" we call them "townies." Both terms can be used neutrally and politely, though they usually aren't. Mostly, it's been fine but, for example, you can't even get a copy of the *New York Times* anywhere on campus, except in the library, where I work; such is the nature of the Midwest.

When my husband and I came here, we had no earthly idea where Thornton was. My husband taught History at Thornton for over 40 years, but we're both from Pennsylvania, originally. He received a professorship here after he got his Ph.D., but, we both had to look at a map to see where in the world we were heading. None of us had any idea we'd spend our entire lives here. It's the kind of place bright, eager people spend a few years in, and then move on, though of course you don't say a thing like that out loud. We just stayed and never left, and I'm not at all unhappy about that. It allowed my husband to teach in the mornings, then do whatever other work or writing he wanted to do the whole rest of the time. And, I've always been involved in the theater here, which has been a lifeline for me.

Thank goodness I've had that outlet over the years! There was never a theater major at Swarthmore, the Quaker College I attended as an undergrad, though now I think they do have one. Contrary to what you might think, there's no disconnect between my being a Quaker and doing theater here. Quakers have mostly been very supportive of the arts, though some segments regard them as frivolous. I would love to have made a career of it, but that just wasn't in the cards. Over time, I worked on a library degree just so we'd have some money; but, my passion has always been the Theater.

The old days at Thornton -- before there even was an established Theater major at the college -- were really the best days, when we had what was known as "The Thornton Players." There wasn't even any credit for it and, of course, no budget, but we had the best time! Even those nights when we had to stay regularly 'till three or four in the morning -- which is kind of standard when you're putting on a play -- we all just loved it. And, we tackled some really ambitions things: Beckett's *Endgame*; Ionesco's *Rhinoceros*; *The Threepenny Opera* -- even *King Lear*. *Lear* was kind of a disaster, actually, but we had a great time trying.

They've killed the Theatre department here at Thornton now because of declining enrollment. Established, then discontinued it, as a major; which is a shame. But, Thornton has had to make tough choices -- make due -- in changing times, just like we all do.

Now that we're inside, I'm just going to write down a few things I need on the wall here with this piece of chalk. You see, we Quaker's try to make everything utilitarian: I don't even use a note pad -- I just jot things on the wall to remember them. Saves on paper!

That's kind of how we've always had to operate here at Thornton. The college was founded by a Presbyterian minister who bought up land, then died before the college could be established. We exist because Lincoln -- *the* Abraham Lincoln -- lost a case in which the state of Illinois was trying to take the land back for Illinois, and the courts said they couldn't do that. He was one of the lawyers on the case, and they lost. Thornton has always been kind of like that: just barely existing, just kind of miraculously here, despite all the odds.

Thornton, as you know, is a strange school, and it takes a special kind of student to work here. You have to work 15 hours a week, and students have even built nine of the twelve buildings on the campus, in addition to working in the Library, the Admin. Building, the Dining Hall, Grounds Crew, Campus Security, etc. You have to be a certain amount broke to come here, but Thornton has always made a virtue of not having enough funds by trying to make the students *make* it work, which is what you do with life: you make a virtue out of necessity. It hasn't always been easy, let me tell you, and it still isn't easy now; but, we get by. I remember my mother squirreling away gold during the depression, saying, after the banks had failed, she wasn't going to let Roosevelt get any of it! That's what I've kind of had to do here my whole life: squirrel away the gold.

It's been a fun atmosphere, actually. There's really nothing else to do here, so the kids have always had to invent their own entertainment. In the early years, you weren't allowed to have a car; there were also still classes on Saturdays, so everyone was always around, and they had to sort of create their own entertainment. But, I mean: our budget was always like $500.00 per play -- some ridiculous amount -- so you were always forced to improvise everything: costumes, sets, you name it.

And, it was an infinitely lively and enthusiastic group. Ask anyone who was around during the time of the Thornton Players, and they'll say they were the liveliest group on campus! Of course, we didn't even have the theater building then. It was just a stage in the gym, and we had to negotiate the space with the basketball team. They've had theater here since the late 1800s -- you can find pictures and programs from way, way back. So, it's an ingrained thing at the school, though now, sadly, it seems to be dying.

When we first met, my husband and I were so poor I had to start taking classes as a librarian, as I said, because the school needed one, and I needed a job; so, there was simply no other way to go. I could have kicked myself later when they added the Theater department, that I hadn't gotten my degree in that. Luckily, the college has always let me direct a play or two a year, even after the department was implemented, simply because I've always done it. Right now, I'm assisting with the school's Madrigal Dinner, and I'm having a dickens of a time with this new, young kid they have over there. They always think they know everything when they come in, and they usually don't. I don't mind, really, but a fellow should know what he's doing before he tries to change everything! They always run the script for the dinner past me to check the *Thee*s and *Thou*s, to make sure they've got them right. It's an outmoded form of speech, of course. Some Quakers still use it, though we don't. But, I grew up hearing it, so I can tell them when they've got it wrong.

It's been another layer of separation from the community to be Quaker here. There's no meeting place for Friends, of course. So, over the years, I simply started going to the Episcopalian church: it just made things easier. Still, there's a bit of a disconnect with the community. We're kind of used to the world not understanding. My husband was a conscientious objector during World War II, and we both wound up volunteering at state mental hospitals, which is what you did then if you were Quaker, or an objector of any kind. Most of the rest of the world didn't respect that choice, of course, and it was hell to be seen around your hometown not in uniform, and you'd always get the questions -- sometimes even verbal abuse. My husband used to say he thought he knew a little bit of what negroes felt like in the south, because he was treated that way. A few years ago, there was a fire in the chapel, which is right where my husband had his office. For a short time, they thought it originated there, and for a brief moment, we wondered whether it might be aimed at my husband, or at our religion. Turns out it *was* connected to religion, just of a different sort: a girl was very distraught about some other matters, and my husband's office just happened to be on the other side of the chapel wall; we've kind of always been on the other side of that wall, in one way or another.

But, we've had a good circle of friends over the years -- mostly other faculty, whom we used to have over to the house regularly (you can see their names written behind the door there, which is something we do when a house is dedicated). And, I sit in on the Shakespeare class sessions on weekends when they read the plays aloud. I just take any part they give me, and it's always amusing to me to see the kids' faces when they look at me, thinking, *What is SHE doing here?* and then I rip into Goneril or Regan, or some such part. It gives them a real jolt, I think, to see this very plainly dressed, unassuming, Quaker woman, demanding Lear give me the part of the kingdom I think is rightly mine!

I love acting, and I know you said you were so impressed to watch Meryl Streep recently in *Sophie's Choice*. There are two schools of thought on that: one is how great it is to watch the actor work; the other is not to notice how effortlessly the actor is doing it. I'm more of the latter camp, myself.

It's just like that movie a while ago, *Tootsie*. Did you see that? I was so disappointed in that film! I wanted to see a real man dealing with how hard it was to make his way in the world, trying to live life as an actual woman, overcoming all the adversities that *real* women face every day. I wish they'd made *that* movie instead, because that would have been really something to see...

OCCLUDED

———◆———

URING GRANT'S FRESHMAN YEAR OF college at Thornton, he was asked to be the guest of some people he didn't know particularly well, on a kind of adventure. The trip was to be a boat ride on the Mississippi River down to Pere Marquette Park, where there was also a plan to camp out overnight. The people were friends of a woman he'd only recently started seeing, named Meg. Grant had reservations not only about the trip, but also about what he was doing by encouraging Meg to think of him as her boyfriend. Still, in the end, his sense of adventure won out, and so -- despite reservations on many different fronts -- he agreed.

Once on the boat, though, the reality of his folly immediately became apparent as the other couples sorted themselves into snuggling duos, arranged variously around the boat. The captain was the father of one of the girls, Melanie Sexton, and Mr. Sexton looked on in good-natured wistfulness as everyone began canoodling in the early autumn sun, the sweatshirts and jeans they'd donned for the short excursion feeling good against the slight chill coming off the murky water of the Mississippi. Grant was new to a situation like this in every way: as someone who had been questioning his sexuality ever since junior high, the expectation that this trip was an invitation to romance now dawned upon him fully, and he began to feel uncomfortable. Grant wasn't certain what he could, or should, be doing; but, as Meg leaned into him, he put his arm around her, in reflex. This felt good and natural, actually, but then, he wasn't sure how much further to take it; nor was he certain Meg wanted much more from him at the moment, either. He felt the warmth of Meg's body pressing into him, could feel the slight curve of her back where her breasts began, and -- because he just assumed this was what a "normal" boyfriend would do -- worked his hand a little closer to the base of her breasts. Again, this felt risky but right and, for a moment, he settled into the mere pleasure of feeling another body pressed against him, no matter whether he was feeling any physical reaction from it or not.

"You have to be really careful of those trees," said Melanie, the captain's daughter, pointing to a particularly ugly stretch of coastline where the jagged tree trunks and half-submerged rocks loomed threateningly from the muddy brown water. "That's not even all of them. A lot of them are under water where you can't see them."

"Really?" said Grant, astonished that the water level could ever rise high enough to cover them, and wondering what else lay submerged just beneath the surface of the swiftly moving waters.

"Yeah, the Mississippi floods all the time. You can see the high-water mark on the grain elevators down in Alton. Half the time, in spring, the whole downtown there is under water."

They had all looked again, amazed to think of the river covering up trees, towns, and even intersections. Just then, Meg looked up and kissed him, and again, Grant was brought literally face-to-face with the reality of where he was, and how he was expected to behave. He returned her kiss, but there was nothing physical stirring at all inside him: he might have been kissing his sister. Still, Grant realized, he was supposed to be her boyfriend. So, after the kiss, he drew Meg even tighter against him.

At one point, as their boat continued between the bluffs, they passed the famed Piasa bird, a vividly colored, red-and-yellow painting on the cliff face in the distance, purportedly done by the long-vanished Cahokia people. The strange and enigmatic drawing had astonished the early explorers Marquette and Joliet on their first trip up the Mississippi. Half dragon, half panther, and with almost Assyrian wings, the symbol had been a mystery to people ever since.

"Is that the Piasa?" said Meg, asking what Grant had been on the verge of asking himself.

"Yeah. They've kind of ruined it, though," said Melanie. "The colors were all fading, and people thought it was being lost, so they made a sort of billboard that sits on top of it. You can't really see the real drawing underneath it anymore -- they completely covered it up."

"I guess they did what they had to do, though," said Grant. He looked at Meg for confirmation, and saw her dark hair parted in the center, her warm brown eyes gazing back at him. *Who was this person he was holding now?* he thought. *What was she expecting from him?* Meg snuggled wordlessly and conspiratorially against him as they watched the sights along the river pass, and he squeezed her in return, his eyes now open and searching the far shore as the force of his hug bent her neck. In order to avoid kissing her on the lips again, he turned sideways and kissed her on the top of her head.

After a long afternoon of much more drifting, they docked in the waning light in the harbor near Pere Marquette. The park had been named after the explorers of these waterways, Father Marquette, who -- presumably -- had been attempting to claim these waters in the name of Christianity and religion. Until just now, as they began to tote their gear (sleeping bags, backpacks full of cooking supplies, etc.), Grant had not thought about the sleeping arrangements very much. When he'd first heard they'd be camping out overnight in sleeping bags, minus tents, just "sleeping under the stars" as Melanie had dreamily advertised it, his first reaction was relief: they'd all be in their own separate sleeping bags, without a tent, so there would be no pressure at all about having sex. However, after observing how close some of the other couples were on the boat that afternoon, the idea occurred to him that, perhaps, Meg would expect him to share her same sleeping bag. Was that possible? And, would any of the other couples have sex with each other, even with the rest of the group within earshot? He had not really anticipated that possibility at all until now.

This nervousness stayed with him even after they'd cooked their meal and set up their sleeping bags, the chill of the evening deepening to the point where some of them were now bundled up in more than one sweatshirt, sweatpants, and even wool socks, as they took to the field to spread their sleeping bags. Grant was pleased the night air was so chilly (surely no one would even think of shucking his or her clothes in such cold, would they?) and watching as the others spread their bags out close to each other, but separate. One couple, who'd been seeing each other for a long time, did indeed, unzip one bag fully, so that it was double, then unzipped the other on top of it, so that it was like a double bed with a comforter on top. However, since they were a long-term couple, Grant breathed a sigh of relief that they were clearly the exception to the rule, and not the norm.

No one was quite ready to go to bed yet and, as the chill deepened, the couples resumed their cuddling postures around the fire, watching the flames lick at the night. It struck Grant that the darkness actually looked deeper just at the point the flames ended, and not, as one might suspect, further up, where a kind of silvered blue seemed to be settling over the earth. Meg leaned up against Grant once again and, this time, kissed him much more passionately. Again, he was brought back hard against the reality of what he was doing. Meg's intensity unnerved him, especially since he could immediately tell he wasn't mirroring it. But, what could he do? He was like an actor trapped in a show whose material he knew wasn't right for him; and yet, the cameras were rolling, the audience was watching, and he knew he was expected to perform a certain role...

Later, lying in the dark beside Meg, each of them safely tucked away in their separate little, sock-like bag, all parts of them thankfully insulated from the cold and everything except a general kind of contact with each other, he lay awake for much of the night, listening to the sounds around them, aware of Meg and her every movement, as she was aware of his. Grant expected she was somewhat disappointed in the way things had gone; still, he didn't get the impression she'd expected things to advance much further than they had. So, they merely lay there, and he could hear the gentle susurrus of the trees, the distant rushing of the water and, now and then, a sharp cry from the woods around them, of an owl or some other bird. *What was it the birds were after?* Grant found himself wondering. *Were they seeking a mate, warning off other suitors, looking for food, or what? Why did their search for partners seem so basic and elemental -- much the way it did for the other couples on the trip -- when, to him, it seemed so alien and strange? Why did everyone seem to want something so entirely different from him, and what was it, exactly, that he wanted? What were these random, vaguely alarming, calls from the darkness all about?*

It was all, ultimately, so unknowable, so obscure...

———◆———

After the trip was over and Grant was back on campus, a friend of his, Todd, asked Grant how it had been, clearly expecting Grant to give him the dirt on whatever kind of shenanigans had presented themselves: who'd had sex with whom, and how far he'd gotten with Meg. Grant played it cool, and told Todd about the trip on the boat, sleeping under the stars -- that sort of thing. Todd clapped Grant on the back good-naturedly, and the feel of Todd's hand, warm and solid on his shoulder, made Grant's groin immediately stiffen. Todd was one of those easy, confident men, and Grant had been aware of a certain attraction toward him in the days and weeks prior. Now, with Todd's hand on his shoulder, and his face close to Grant's, the reaction in Grant was volcanic and immediate -- nothing at all like what he'd felt over the weekend toward Meg.

"So, did you and Meg do the nasty?" said Todd impishly, his face alarmingly close to Grant's.

"What, with all those other people around?" said Grant, deflecting both the question and the physical reaction taking place inside him, which was completely hidden from Todd -- as hidden as the tree trunks they'd drifted over in the boat when they were on the Mississippi.

Later that month, when they were all going home for break, Todd took Grant to the Amtrak station, and stood waiting as Grant boarded and moved into the center of the car. The glass must have looked tinted from the outside because, as Grant waved at Todd enthusiastically from inside the train, Todd looked right though and past him.

Apparently, Grant realized, Todd wasn't able to see him at all.

"HEY, MAN, WHERE YOU AT?"

———————

THE SUMMER AFTER HIS FRESHMAN year in college, after weeks of searching, Justin Lloyd finally found a job at the local paper, delivering newspaper bundles to the local carriers for distribution on their routes. It was a night-shift job, when most of the rest of the world was asleep and, in the sleepy country towns and rural areas around his hometown of Moline, it essentially meant he could ignore any and all traffic laws and road signs. Thus, Justin often found himself blowing through stop signs at deserted intersections in the small, blue hours before the dawn, driving the wrong way up one-way streets, and parking in the center of the street for a short time to fill the metal newsstands with the *Moline Daily Times*. Because the absence of any traffic and the curious suspension of traffic laws gave him a great deal of time to think, he often found himself dreaming and speculating, and was deriving a certain pleasure from being able to flaunt certain accepted norms. He had only recently begun to come to terms with his sexuality, and was still uncertain about a number of things. At the end of the school year, he'd met a classmate named Tom, who'd helped him get over his initial fear and indecision about being gay; he was also still trying to deal with the fallout of his attraction for his closest friend, Kyle.

As positive as Tom's influence had been, though, the summer had intervened, Justin had returned to Moline in order to find a job, and Tom had returned to his family and a small, farming community outside Bloomington. He and Tom had spoken to each other several times since school ended, but they still hadn't managed to get together. Lately, Justin's new-found confidence was wavering, and he'd found himself, at times, intently pondering Bible passages that explicitly condemned homosexuality, especially the Leviticus verse which read: "Thou shalt not lie with man as with a woman. It is abomination." He was also reading and trying to understand the story of Sodom and Gomorrah. He felt a healthy dose of fear in looking at these passages, and yet was reasonably certain he didn't put much credence in them. After all, why would God create a whole class of men and women damned because of who they loved? Wasn't love, after all, a good thing? At other times, he rooted around in secret in the few books he could find: *Homosexuals in History*, and *Everything You've Always Wanted to Know About Sex, But Were Afraid to Ask* -- books whose sense of homosexuality was basically to diagnose it as a pathology -- and found himself feeling more and more free to reject them. Still, the isolation was beginning to take its toll, and he fluctuated daily between an attitude of confidence, and one of total doubt.

At work, he was surrounded by a group of high school dropouts, all of whom seemed equally as remote as he must have seemed to them, and who regarded him like a creature from another planet.

"Someday, when you make a million dollars, I'll come look you up," said Tommy to him hopefully one day. Tommy was short and squat, with a faint, scraggly black mustache vaguely reminiscent of a Civil War-era daguerreotype.

For a second, Justin wasn't certain what Tommy meant. Then, when he realized Tommy thought that, since he was going to college, he'd be rich, he wasn't certain how to respond. The question seemed naive and sad, and Justin merely said, "Yeah, don't hold your breath for that."

"What, ain't you college boys all supposed to wind up rich? Ain't that the point?" said Tommy, looking somewhat disappointed.

"For some, I guess," he said. "Not for me."

"What are you going for, then?" said Tommy, looking even more perplexed.

"Just to learn," said Justin, lamely. "I don't know. I want to be a writer someday." He felt stupid saying this, and figured this response would likely set him even further away from this group of guys; and yet, he wasn't sure what else to say.

"Shit," said Tommy with surprising gentleness, then ambled off to load his truck.

Justin was conscious of a strange affection and attraction toward the guys he worked with at the newspaper. On weekend nights, they'd circle up the vans and drink a beer or two before they headed out on their runs. In a hollow off the highway, they'd sit for an hour or more and shoot the breeze, the five of them condensing into the intimacy of two vans, pulled side-by-side. Sometimes, a joint, which Justin always passed along untried, traveled down the circle; sometimes, they just sat wordlessly, the insects buzzing in the country summer air. He felt protected -- safe -- among these men, some of whom were, indeed, men, being in their late twenties or even early thirties. He felt this way despite thinking that, in another context, one or two of them would likely be the kind of guys who'd beat the shit out of him if they knew about his sexuality. For the most part, though, even with the difference between their worlds, he felt a bond with them, and was more than a little amazed and flattered they'd accepted him as much as they had.

One night, as Justin was getting ready for his run, Chad stopped by the paper on his night off, just to visit with the guys. Chad was Justin's favorite of the group: thin and tanned, with long blond hair, Chad was like a surfer boy in some respects, save that he was 1500 miles inland. Somehow, though, this fit his personality as well, since Chad always seemed just a little dazed and lost. There was a gentleness about Chad, though, which Justin found appealing. That, coupled with Chad's adventurous and open personality, had made Justin wonder whether Chad might be bisexual, or at least someone he could talk to about his own emerging sexuality. He felt that Chad, in contrast to the other guys, would not freak out or judge him if he hinted he was gay -- not that he'd tell him everything that had happened with Tom, of course. Justin thought he could probably trust Chad with an admission about being gay -- though, on this score, he was a bit afraid: he was the new guy, after all, just there to work the summer. Chad might not feel as loyal to him as he obviously felt toward all the other guys, and things might not go well if the word were to get out about him.

Up to this point, Justin had never really spent much time alone with Chad. Tonight, however, Chad said, "Hey, Justin, buddy, how 'bout dropping me at my girlfriend's house? It's not too far off your route."

"Sure," said Justin, though he knew it was against company rules to use a vehicle for personal errands.

Now, as they hopped into the van and headed out, Justin took in Chad's long, lanky body as he slumped down in his seat and lit a cigarette. Chad wore a bright red, tank-top t-shirt that showed off his tan. Justin noticed again his lean-ness, and saw the small blond bush of hair underneath his arms. Chad cupped both his hands around his cigarette and sucked, the lighter's flame now shadow-ing his cheek and lower jaw. There was a comfortable maleness about Chad, an effortless and attractive niceness. Chad was slumped down in his seat, his back against the door, legs splayed wide toward Justin, and Justin felt an easy intimacy with him. As they chatted of this and that, Justin kept wondering how to bring up the subject of his sexuality. How did one jump into a thing like that?

Then, as they rode and Chad sat next to him so unselfconsciously, Justin almost wondered whether Chad might feel the same attraction he did. Chad was sitting very close to him, after all -- so close that his legs occasionally bumped Justin's, each time giving Justin a little thrill.

"So, Justin," said Chad. "You got a girlfriend, man?"

Justin looked at Chad and, rather than the usual fear or guardedness he might have felt upon hearing someone ask him this -- especially someone he felt attracted to -- he felt a spark of hope flare up: the smallest, weakest light of pos-sibility. It was the way Chad asked it: not as though it were the usual assumption, but instead, an actual question, with a multiplicity of possible answers.

Justin looked at Chad, his face lit by the dimness of the dashboard lights, the darkness of the country rushing past behind him. He almost thought he *did* see a hint of questioning in the eyes -- the hint of something unsure hovering around his full, red lips.

"No," said Justin, his heart pounding now, aware of entering dangerous ter-ritory. "No, I don't." He wondered to himself if it were possible that this was it -- that here, at last, was the moment he'd been waiting for: the moment he might finally take Chad into his confidence. And, if he did so, might Chad admit he was gay as well? Might Chad even be attracted to him? What might *that* lead to? And how would he react if that *were* to happen? What about Tom?

"Oh, come on now," said Chad. "A big, good-looking, college-type like you?" He took a drag and looked at Justin warmly, affably.

Justin wasn't certain what to think. Was Chad flirting with him after all? He was aware of an erection beginning, and the nervousness and excitement of this scenario made him feel like stopping the van right then and throwing himself into Chad's arms. Instead, the countryside continued whipping past as Justin weighed his options. All Chad had asked was whether he had a girlfriend. Possibly, it was as innocent as that. And yet, to Justin, the air of the van felt like a force-field of electrical currents.

"Yeah, right," said Justin. "Me, good looking?"

To his disappointment now, Chad did not contradict him. Instead, he took another long drag on his cigarette, its lit end glowing like a black-edged poppy in the dark, then sat there in the silence without saying anything additional.

Casting about for something to say, some way to revive the thread, Justin risked flirtatiousness, and said, "Maybe if I looked like *you*." He allowed the thought to trail off, to let Chad make of it whatever he wanted.

"Shit," said Chad, exhaling in an "aw, shucks" manner.

Justin felt the smoke caress his cheek -- air that had just been in Chad's lungs -- and breathed it in. He watched Chad stare off into the interstices of the trees, the darkness in which nothing could be seen, then said hopefully: "I bet you could have just about anyone you want." He meant this both as compliment and invitation.

Chad, however, seemed to keep ignoring all his bait. "Oh, hell yes," he said. "I just have to beat 'em off with a stick."

Justin couldn't think what to say. He could feel the momentum ebbing, slipping past, and wasn't certain how to rescue it. He watched Chad dig in his pocket and produce a joint: white paper rolled and twisted like a cloth hair curler.

"Hey, man. You mind if I do this?"

"No," said Justin, startled to discover that he truly didn't. They were miles away from anywhere and anyone, and the likelihood of being caught was nil. Besides, he thought, as Chad lit up: perhaps Chad's getting high was good. Perhaps the conversation would eventually drift to what he really wanted to talk about. Perhaps, if Chad got high, the long-sought sharing of his fears -- the hoped-for connection he hoped to find -- would suddenly occur.

But, as he watched Chad get even mellower, somehow he knew it wasn't going to happen. After several tokes, Chad picked up the radio, which all the vans used to stay in contact with each other, and intoned in a comic drone: *"Moline Daily Times* vehicles, all *Moline Daily Times* vehicles, report your status."

There was a pause, a few crackles, then Justin recognized Tommy's voice saying, "Chad, is that you?"

"10-4, good buddy," said Chad, grinning impishly. "We got a copy."

"Who the hell you freeloading off of tonight, you motherfucker?" said Tommy, laughing.

"That'd be my good buddy, Justin," said Chad, grinning down into the microphone. There was a pause, some blasts of country static, then again, the voice of Tommy:

"Hey, Justin, dump that worthless load of shit you got beside you out onto the road with all your other bundles, man."

Suddenly, the other vans were joining in on the harangue, and Justin listened, smiling, though he could feel the intimacy he and Chad had shared slipping irrevocably away.

"Hey, man, where you at?" said Tommy finally, that final preposition jarring Justin, so he almost missed Chad's reply.

"We're just coming off bush hill and heading down into muff hollow."

Chad winked at Justin now, and Justin slowly realized the sexual innuendo. He heard the hooting from the other vans, and saw Chad smiling slyly, though the smile seemed like a leer now, and the hippy, dopey quality Justin thought was so attractive moments ago, in the intimacy of the van, now seemed different to him: sadder and more ridiculous.

"Whoa, man," said Chad suddenly, like someone starting from a reverie. "Hang a louie here."

As the car pulled off the road and Chad directed him up the street to his girlfriend's house, Justin could feel the whole episode coming to an abrupt, unsatisfying end.

"Give my best to Cassie," leered Tommy suggestively as he signed off on the radio to Chad.

"Yeah, don't you wish," said Chad, hanging up the mouthpiece. "Thanks, man," he said to Justin, exiting the car. "You're a gentleman and a scholar."

Justin watched Chad's trim figure disappearing into the darkness with a mixture of disappointment and relief. He turned the car around to get back on the road, glanced back at all the newspaper bundles in the back of the van, and felt the emptiness descending on him once again: all his cargo still there, and all of it still waiting to be unloaded.

———————

One evening, when he wasn't working the night shift, Justin took the family car and headed out to a writer's group he'd heard about. Moline was an old, river town on the banks of the Mississippi. It had a kind of faded charm, and certain sections of it overlooked the Mississippi River, moving dull and brown below. Mostly, though, it was a sleepy, fairly conservative, Midwestern town, with not a lot of room for people who did not fit into clearly defined norms. The writer's group was in an older part of town that had once housed the wealthiest people; now, some of the mansions had been turned into public spaces, including one that had become a civic center. As he pulled into the parking lot adjacent to white-trellised gardens lush with a profusion of pink petunias in full midsummer growth, it all felt unfamiliar, strange. He'd visited the place before, but never in the guise of an aspiring writer, and he felt like an imposter being here: restless, uncomfortable, and out-of-place, as he had all summer long.

Now, as he made his way down huge, grey, passageways that carved out the interior space in a somewhat disorienting manner, he found the room scheduled for the meeting and waited nervously as the other writers -- some young, some old, all in comfortable summer clothing -- filtered in. Doubting himself again, he wondered whether he should leave. Who were these people -- who was *he* -- to be here, thinking they could write?

Yet, as he sat there, Justin knew -- or thought he knew -- that this was where he needed to be. He'd come armed with a manuscript that was very influenced by a novel he'd recently read called *The Paths of the Sea,* by Pierre Schoendoerfer. The novel was about a man trying to understand his life-long friendship with another man -- a friendship that both haunted and goaded him into trying to figure out who he really was, and what, exactly, he felt toward his friend. Justin wasn't sure what the group would think of it, or even if he'd get a chance to read. Fortunately, as the group commenced and the people introduced themselves, the moderator, who resembled Justin's high school Social Studies teacher (indeed, the man turned out to be a teacher, though his area was History), asked Justin if he'd like to read, since he was new.

"It's almost 7 pages," said Justin, apologetically.

"That's not that long," said the moderator, whose name was Chuck. "Go ahead. We'll stop you if we need to."

When Justin had finished reading, he glanced up nervously around the room.

After a silence of a few more moments, Chuck said, "Well, group: what do we think?"

A heavy-set woman with a style sense frozen somewhere in the '50s -- henna-haired, with thick, black, plastic glasses -- ventured at last: "It sounds like Jay Gatsby."

"The writing, or the character?" asked someone else, a middle-aged man in a rumpled, white work shirt.

"Both," said the red-haired woman, seemingly intent on being brilliant, and yet not certain whether she'd achieved it.

"I think the language and the character are good," said a man who'd introduced himself as a poet. "But, you lost me with the story somewhere along the way. I think you need more action in it. You need to get outside the man's head a bit." Justin had been looking at this man before the meeting started, wondering if there were any possibility he might be gay. Now that the man had made these comments, however, Justin found himself resenting his broad shoulders and good looks, concluding that he was -- like Chad -- likely a disreputable womanizer.

"What was that part where it almost sounded like he was in love with his friend?" said someone else -- a woman who looked like she could be a social worker of some kind. "I think that part could have been heightened and explored a little bit further."

Justin cringed at this -- wished, suddenly, that he could flee. The rest of the comments ran the gamut from encouragement to puzzlement and, as he left the meeting that night, Justin felt discouraged.

At his car, however, Chuck caught up with him.

"How'd you feel about all the feedback?" said Chuck.

"Well, I guess I've got a lot to learn," said Justin, meekly. He almost wished he hadn't come, and yet, some of the people had been fairly supportive.

"Listen, don't take it too much to heart," said Chuck. "Those people are fine with some kinds of writing but, for more literary stuff like yours..." He let his thoughts taper off, and Justin merely stood, uncertain what to say.

"I think your story's really good," said Chuck. "Don't listen too much to what they say. Just keep at it, and I think someday you'll really have something there. Your character is just confused about where he's at."

Once again, Justin felt the jar of the final preposition in that phrase, "Where he's at," and wondered, as he had with Chad: why didn't people just simply say, "Where he *is*?" or why Tommy hadn't asked that night, "Where *are* you?" He guessed they liked the emphasis of that final "at," but it always rang oddly in his ear.

Then, suddenly, Justin was aware of how close Chuck was standing -- of a curious insistence in his presence beside him at the car. Chuck was wearing a lime-green *Adidas* t-shirt that accentuated a stocky build, white running shorts, and long, white socks pulled almost to the knee. Looking now at Chuck, he felt a certain awareness building within himself -- a curious, sexually tinged tension.

"Thanks," said Justin, reaching for the car door nervously, although he didn't open it.

"Listen, are you here for the summer?" asked Chuck, a little too eagerly.

Justin wasn't certain what to say. All he knew was that, right now, from the vibrations he was getting off Chuck, something larger and more definite was imminent. Suddenly petrified about what might be happening, he hedged:

"Yeah, but not that much longer. I mean, I'm heading back to college in a little while."

"Oh. Well, I hope you come back to the group again," said Chuck, a bit crestfallen.

They stood for a moment, and Justin knew he should say he'd return but, right now, he was thinking there was no way he'd be back again next week. He didn't know whether his piece showed any talent or not; he wasn't even certain what it meant. All he knew was that Chuck's presence beside him felt dangerously, threateningly sexual, and he wasn't certain what to do.

"I'll try," said Justin, finally.

"Listen, let me give you my number" said Chuck, undaunted, ripping off a half-sheet of paper from the stack he held beneath his arms. "If you ever feel like getting together sometime, give me a call."

"Sure," said Justin, taking the paper from him and opening the car door. As he did so, he flashed on the character at the end of his short story, looking bewildered at his name on the credit card in his hand. Feeling suddenly surreal, he looked up at Chuck, and the thick, bushy mustache hanging above his upper lip. Reeling now, he focused on it, trying desperately to root himself somewhere in space and time.

THE DANDELION CLOUD

JOHN HAYES KEPT DRIVING THROUGH the Illinois countryside, even though he knew his mission was absurd. Flustered and somewhat ashamed of himself for even being in his car and following through with such a ridiculous proposition, he found himself almost wishing that the friend he had agreed to meet at the dandelion field twenty years after college graduation would not be there.

It really is quite unfair of me to expect him to remember, he thought; and yet, of course, he still hoped -- still believed, deep down -- that Kent would meet him there.

He had been driving all day, persisting blindly toward that field, fulfilling his part of the long-forgotten promise as much from a sense of loyalty to the halcyon days of his youth as to an unflagging sense of curiosity. Would Kent, indeed, remember the promise, and meet him as they'd planned?

It had all been so long ago! And yet, now, as he thought of it, not long ago at all. The whims of youth, the lotus-eating quality of college days, passing in a state so much like a dream that, at times, he'd had to stop and think in order to reassure himself that an event in question had actually taken place. Once, for instance, he'd been walking with Kent through fields in early spring, the sun full and the fields just newly plowed. The depths of hues that day had been astonishing: the air did not dissolve the lines of things in rising waves of heat. Everything had seemed suffused with rightness then! The sun shone down on every object in its place, and he felt absolutely grounded -- absolutely present -- in the fresh-washed light.

Seeing it there all of a sudden had made them stop. The huge, white mass swirled in front of them in such an innocent-yet-foreign manner that, at first, they'd had trouble comprehending what it was. Because it strained the limits of credulity, really. Yet, the cloud of dandelion seeds was there in front of them, its movement unbelievable and -- as they watched it rotate, slowly and heavily -- even slightly hideous. Certainly, each of them had seen dandelions blowing in the wind; had picked them as a child, gingerly, in order not to knock off any of the fragile seeds; had held them gently, puffing either a short burst of air or a long, steady stream in order for the seeds to do their weightless *tour jete*: the slow free-fall. Each had, indeed, seen expansive fields covered with the weeds; and yet, neither of them had ever imagined such a quantity of seeds amalgamated in one place.

The cloud continued moving sickeningly in front of them -- caught up within a large exhaust vent -- and, in an instant, he was saddened. Thinking back to all those childhood memories -- to the simple innocence of wishes bestowed upon each airborne seed -- he'd felt outraged by this ugly mass, silenced by the hopeless struggle of it as he watched the seeds strain to free themselves from the current that entrapped them, fail, and then get dashed down roughly to the greasy asphalt of the parking lot. It seemed, somehow, so far removed from the startling, yellow assertion of life and spring each simple, sunny dot had once represented, he had resolved silently that this cloud had nothing at all to do with the flash of summer, youth, or wishes borne on air.

For John Hayes, college life had been a revelation, unexpected and profound: a liberation from the tepidness of life lived within the stultifying confines of tradition and propriety; an initiation into freedom and honesty; and a welcome plunge into days made bright by spontaneity and love. Meeting his friend, Kent, had immediately underscored for John how passionless and sad his life had been up to this point -- how utterly unquestioning and predetermined everything about it was: a life devoid of all discussion and decision (even the need for it), since everything was either known, insinuated, or assumed. As he reflected on it now, he thought that all his life, in fact, had been lived rather blindly and obediently, carried out without a sense of purpose overarching what he now saw as the whole, vast charade that was existence: no goals hinted at on the horizon that would have given the vision any kind of unity or meaning, as though following a bad play to its anti-climactic denouement. In college, though, he'd found the nerve to walk out on the play -- to get up and abandon it in favor of a script and characters that seemed more authentic. With Kent, he'd improvised a role and let it grow for four years straight, and it had been the highlight of his life.

Now, however, as he stopped to analyze the present, he discovered that that imagined role seemed to have gotten lost somewhere along the line -- that he and it had parted company, and he had drifted back into complacency, inaction, and despair. Now, as he looked back on his life, he found that only college friends stood out as bright spots on the grey, undifferentiated plain of retrospect. All dappled in the sunlight in his mind, they stood as still and mute as Grecian statuary in the foliage, caught up in awkward poses of those long-past days. Over the years, in reminiscence, as he'd paused in front of this or that frozen, half-clad figure, he'd been struck by waves of emptiness and regret -- a feeling that was always so endemic to the contemplation of his past. It was like walking through an empty town, or when he'd visited the ruins of Pompeii, or strolled about the gardens in Grenada. All had in common that same feeling of a great thing lost -- an age long dead, when men lived lives of leisure and of beauty; when sunlit days were spent in flower-trellised shade, and dime-thin books of poetry were read in cool and fountained grottoes. This melancholy garden of remembrance was his own Theogony: the place where memories become mythologized, and friends preserved forever. This was his bittersweet Gethsemane as well, though -- like that famous garden -- this place, too, was one where souls, once watchful, were inclined to fall asleep, their inattentiveness leading to the ultimate betrayal.

At times -- especially the last few years -- he worried that, if he'd not exactly been inattentive, he'd at least been guilty of a kind of somnambulism; that he'd fallen back into a life of emptiness, and had not continued with the kind of life he saw the gateway to in those years at school with Kent. Indeed, he hadn't spoken to Kent now in a dozen years -- hadn't spoken to him all that much, really, since they'd graduated, though he couldn't, for the life of him, have said why, especially given how much Kent had meant to him all these years. Pained at this thought, and caught up again in the clutches of his recent, recurring doubt, he found himself again confronted with the thought he'd had so often through the years -- that nagging thought of how complete he might have been if he had simply died in some freak accident immediately after college, or if he'd put a bullet through his head. The years of dissoluting loneliness and pain he might have saved if he had only done so! Once again, he felt a stab of emptiness that wouldn't let the conflict rest, yet wondered, in the next breath, if that was truly how he felt, why he should now feel such an urge to yank his car off of its present course and head toward home? Why, he asked himself, if he cherished Kent and all those college days so much, should he feel this hesitancy and fear?

Suddenly, reflecting upon this, he felt the doubt about his mission yielding to a sense of hope. Why should he, after all, be so afraid of going back? This was a trip, after all, to reconnect with Kent -- this friend who'd brought such meaning to his life!

He thought back now to the ways Kent had been supportive all those years ago, going back particularly to the night he'd received the news about his father. John's father was a good deal older than most of his friends' parents, so that he had never really formed the type of bonds one would expect with a father -- knew him very distantly and fearfully, indeed, this bank fund manager whose plane had gone down in a fog somewhere, and whose corporeal remains -- perhaps ironically -- were never to be found. John recollected talking to his mother quietly, a quietness his mother received with her usual restraint, and which Kent had attributed to shock, but which had really arisen from the emptiness he'd always felt whenever he thought about his family. It wasn't that John had been indifferent to his father: merely that he'd never known him. Even now, he still could feel the guilt about his lack of grief; and yet, the guilt had only served to deepen his ambivalence. His only certain thought that night was of the anticlimax of the whole thing -- of how much he hated the reserve his mother showed: she, in her dead, dull monotone, reciting the funeral date and time. He somehow longed for someone closer to be dead (*and yet*, he wondered, *who could that possibly have been*? He'd never really been that close to anyone but Kent), if only for the luxury of feeling grief -- of having known, by that, that there had once been love! He longed for the catharsis of tears, for falling into stronger arms: the total letting go.

Kent had been beside him that night and, as they talked, John had been fascinated and astonished by the apparent ease and earnestness of Kent's sympathy. He tried to think how Kent might have acted if *Kent* had been the one to get this news, remembering acutely, now, the nature and affection that always seemed to mark Kent's interactions with his family. John felt certain, if the roles had been reversed, Kent would really have been crushed, and Justin was sure this was one of the reasons he loved Kent so: Kent had brought into his life a real example of what love was, and what it meant. As he had looked at Kent that night, he'd noticed once again Kent's vigor and solidity, the absolute and undeniable sexual authority of him. Reaching out timidly to touch Kent on the back, he'd marveled at the firmness of the features that so dwarfed his own. Kent always seemed to be feeling a spontaneous happiness toward life that John could never share. He seemed anchored, somehow, in some fundamental base of feeling that he, himself, had never been able to access.

Patting John on the shoulders as if to emphasize their camaraderie -- not so much trying to cheer him up as to extend a hand to someone who so obviously and desperately seemed to need it -- Kent had taken him out to a bar. Putting his arms around John, gathering him together, really, trying to bolster him up, Kent had urged him to let go. Yet, strangely, he remembered feeling not a release in the face of all this selfless intimacy but, instead, a strange self-consciousness and fear. There, in the midst of this embrace, with Kent's arms around him, strongly, masculinely, securely locking Justin against that bearlike chest; with Kent's beard against his shoulder, and Kent's warm breath upon his ear, he'd almost felt...he had the sense -- well, really, that was probably the closest he had ever come to love. Of course, he'd never told Kent this: it wouldn't do to complicate their friendship in that way. And yet, somehow, he always wondered how it might have changed things if he had.

Sitting in the yellow light of the bar later on that same evening after getting the news about his father, the world becoming pleasantly fuzzy, he'd felt a flush of love, gratitude, and security steal over him. He was propped up in the booth between the wall and Kent, his buddy (he'd used the word far too many times that night), there on the aisle side, protecting him from falling out or into pieces. He had let his eyes go wandering among the shadows of the room and come to the conclusion that the world was full of a staggering amount of solitude and silence sometimes. It wasn't just the shadows and the silence in the bar or in himself: he'd felt it many times before. He thought again about the stillness of the campus late at night: a silence that was not dispelled by chapel bells, but heightened -- deepened -- by their tolling. Sometimes, walking across the campus alone after being at the bar -- clinging to the last, slow minutes of the night as one holds fast to dreams -- he would snap awake and find himself stopped in his tracks, his body fixed and purposeful, aware that bells were ringing now, and yet, uncertain of the count. He'd wait until he thought the chimes were done, then stand there for a moment more, as if he hoped to hear just one more toll. As the seconds passed, he'd grow amused and turn toward home; and yet, he knew the silence of that missing toll was like the silence that had been there all his life -- those sounds and words you hoped to hear someday, but never did. Words like: "Your life means something." "You're important." Or, "Your mother and I love you."

Entering his room after one such night, he had immediately turned on all the lights, then cursed the fact that the overhead bulb wasn't stronger. There always seemed to be a kind of pall -- a weak bleakness -- at the heart of its illumination. Shivering involuntarily, he felt again the stillness of the freezer-like cold of the recent walk, recalled how -- so often, in walking across the campus -- he'd noticed that the spotlights mounted on the eaves of the buildings always seemed to light the faces coming toward him in the dark, yet never his. He contemplated all this many times in the half-light of his room, in the library or at the bar; but all that bleakness and darkness had been dispelled by Kent. He had entered John's life during those college years, and it was as though Kent had drawn back all the curtains, and he could finally feel the sun.

With graduation, though, all that had ended: all that closeness had been petrified by time. Perhaps it was the distance that had fallen in between them, or the fact that one can only travel so far down the road of other people's lives. He wasn't sure, but it had happened, despite that optimistic, graduation day promise: "What do you say we promise to meet each other again in 20 years, right out at that field where we saw the dandelion cloud that day?"

Even still at school, he'd caught a whiff of it. Near the very end of school, he'd gotten so despondent, he had taken refuge in the chapel, only to discover that a girl from one of his classes was there already, practicing a piece he'd always loved. It was a Chopin Nocturne, Opus 27, No. 1 and, as he sat down, unperceived, to listen to her play, he heard again the reasons he had always loved it: long and supple lines of elegant, quietly expressed, emotion, and a melody that wandered, with a seeming aimlessness, until it harmonized with other lines in unexpected ways; the whole piece moving with a kind of melancholy to a center section which, he now remembered, he had never liked: a kind of dance, mazurka-like and crass, that crept in unexpectedly and took the piece in another direction until, at last, the noise and clamoring subsided, and the piece returned again to the gentle, expressive strains of the opening. He'd sat there listening anew, it seemed, to how the piece was ending, building with a sense of resoluteness to a final chord, which -- when it came -- backed unexpectedly from *forte* down to *pianissimo*.

The girl then began to take up problematic sections of the work; however, as he listened to it again, it suddenly struck him very differently, and he wondered why he'd always liked it so much. It seemed to him, upon listening to it this time, that he'd caught some anticlimax in the whole -- a sense, almost, of ineffectuality -- which he'd never heard before. He felt now about the piece much the same way he'd always felt about the *Offertoire* of Faure's *Requiem*: that same magnificence and beauty at the opening, its melodies suffused with supplication, regret, and sorrow; pleading in the face of all eternity for understanding; absolution; rest. Yet, the central solo always seemed, somehow, so uninspired and dull. He longed to live within the passion of that opening, much the way he'd always longed to live within the passages of books. He thought of all the times he'd stared at pages, words, the ink on paper -- looked at the gap between the words, and marveled at the way the eye could scan it all and change it swiftly into thought. Communication: how he envied it! And passion: how he wanted that! How had he wound up here? Here, in a center section that he didn't like? And she -- the girl. She didn't even know that he was there!

He had left the chapel then, upset, half wanting her to notice him and call out -- make him stay: it seemed to him they all had so little time left before everything changed! And yet, he had departed noiselessly, of course, not wanting to disturb her. He pulled the door closed quietly behind him, and tried to escape without a sound.

It was the kind of incident that paralleled his whole life. He had always had that sense of drifting deaf and mute through crowds; aching to express and yet unable; moving through the currents of his longing like some gravid and exhausted salmon. He recalled the fantasy he'd always had of meeting someone in a foreign country after years of isolation; lapsing into English after years of never speaking it; falling back into a mother tongue like falling back on dreams. He'd taken Latin all through school -- had felt a twinge of sorrow and regret whenever classmates, who'd taken French or Spanish, began to speak to foreigners unhesitatingly. And yet, he still felt he would not have done it any other way -- could not, and still find himself driving down the highway to this dandelion field to meet an age-old friend; to find out whether youthful promises held true, and whether love endured.

Rounding a corner in sight of the agreed-upon meeting place (*The empty dandelion field was still there, after all these years!*), He felt his heart rise in his chest, and pushed his foot a little harder to the floor, anticipating -- straining through the dust to see if Kent had come. Seeing no one, however, he pulled his car into the far edge of the gas station parking lot and shut the motor off: he was prepared to wait.

———◆———

When the afternoon was through, John decided to buy some gas before the station closed, and then look for a hotel. After he filled his gas tank, the attendant asked him for his credit card and, as he handed the man his card, John took a good, long look at the soiled white strip with his signature upon it. Staring like that, uncomprehending, he made the gas station attendant suspicious.

"Anything wrong, mister? This *is* your card, right?"...

John nodded vaguely, then walked into the field behind the station. In the middle of the dandelions then, he looked up toward the sky and ached with the desire to be transmuted deep into the blankness of its hue. He stood for hours, unmoving, feeling disbelievingly the contents of his pockets, knowing Kent would never come. As he stood there now, he felt confirmed within his bowels the truth of what he'd been afraid of all along: that he'd lived a life of cowardice and regret, which had in no way prepared him for the reality stretched in front of him -- for winds that blew across the plains from worlds as vacant and as barren as the one that now confronted him.

(for Kyle and Craig, who would have come)

THE MOMENT

———◆———

"Do people really understand what it means to caress someone?"

PATRICIA NELL WARREN, *THE FRONT RUNNER*

B RAD HAD BEEN CAPTIVATED BY Paul from the day he first saw him but, of course, at Thornton College, in the middle of rural Illinois in 1979, there was no way for him to acknowledge -- let alone act on -- that feeling. Brad had come here to this small town increasingly aware of his attraction to men, but also, painfully aware he had chosen perhaps the least-promising location in the world ever to be able to act upon and explore that desire. His room was located on the ground floor of a low-slung, red-brick dorm at this small, liberal arts college with a miniscule student body, and his window looked out over the track and soccer fields. At the far edge of campus lay vast tracts of corn and soybean fields; soccer nets strained the wind in the nearer distance. Every day, he could hear the whistles and look out his window to see the team practicing. The first time he caught sight of Paul, practicing in his navy blue shorts: blond-haired, shirtless, there was something in the form and shape of him that Brad could not stop looking at, the way one can't quite get enough of watching animals in the wild, or some other creature totally at home in its natural environment.

Brad was surprised that first time, after watching him, to see Paul come trotting into their dorm after practice; he had not realized Paul lived on his floor. Paul had waved happily and sweatily at him, exuberant and boisterous after an exhausting afternoon session, and Brad could still remember the late-August warmth in the dorm floors, with the doors and windows propped open, the drowsy din of stereo music playing, and the sweaty smell of boys permeating the dorm.

"Hey," said Paul, breezing past him and continuing down the hall five doors away from his, and across the other side of the dingy hallway.

"Hey," said Brad shyly, watching the figure retreat and disappear into the square of light of his own room, so close and yet so far away. Even the merest acknowledgement by Paul brought him a little thrill and, as he stood in the small, lopsided square of light savoring it, he felt suddenly electrified to be in such close proximity to someone so beautiful.

That evening, he saw Paul in the cafeteria, and Paul surprised him by saying cheerfully, "Hey, you're my neighbor!"

"Yeah, I live just down the hall from you."

"Cool," said Paul. "I'm Paul."

"Brad. I saw you out at soccer practice. My room looks out over the field."

"Yeah, I'm out there pretty much every afternoon. Hey," said Paul, apparently mistaking Brad's interest for a similar interest in athletics, "You wanna maybe work out together sometime?"

"Do I look like I work out?" said Brad, flinching, as usual, from any contact with sports.

"I don't know," said Paul, with surprising innocence. "Maybe, maybe not."

What had just happened was what Brad dreaded most: the presumption of seemingly every male in the world that *all* males were somehow interested in sports, or in the development of their bodies. Brad was interested in neither -- or rather, he was unfailingly interested in the development of the bodies of *other* men, and always felt shy and self-conscious about his own. Reflexively, he concluded now that Paul's interest in him was essentially over, and stood for a moment awkwardly.

"So, is that a yes or a no?" said Paul, looking at him with an earnestness that somehow obviated all of Brad's fears of ridicule and inadequacy, and made him want to take a chance.

"Okay, sure," he said, "but, I don't know very much about it."

"No problem," said Paul. "Why don't you come over to the gym with me after dinner?"

After that, they made a number of trips together across the end-of-summer quad to the antediluvian, 1950s-style, yellow-brick gym, dark, lumbrous, and quiet at this time of night. Paul showed him how to use the various equipment and, as he sat and did chest presses on the Nautilus (leg lifts, curls, and the like), Brad had mimicked his movements, timidly at first, and with much smaller weights, yet with a growing sense of confidence and support. Always, he tried not to look too longingly at the various muscles and fibers striating and contracting in Paul's arms and legs, and also, not to be too self-conscious about his own weakness. What encouraged and amazed him was how Paul seemed honestly thrilled about discovering the power of his own body, continually challenging himself; and yet, he was not competitive or belittling of Brad's weakness. Indeed, his enthusiasm was infectious, and he was always wildly encouraging about even Brad's smallest successes.

Nightly, after they had been together, Brad would lie in his sultry dorm room, flushed with the elation of this unexpected new bond, recounting the ways he and Paul had interacted with each other, and remembering the way Paul's arms and legs and chest had looked on each and every exercise. Paul was so unselfconscious about his body, so free with hugs and slaps that sometimes Brad even wondered whether Paul might mirror his attraction in some way. Speculating on this possibility led him to endless reveries, and he could hardly sleep due to his wonder and excitement. Yet, to cross that line and take a chance meant risking everything. So, he lay there nightly, remembering, speculating, and burning with want.

One day, after they'd been going to the gym together for about two weeks, he was struggling to lift more weight than he was really capable of, and Paul said to him: "You're going to have to build up your shoulders and back some more before you can really begin to work on the arms and chest."

As he spoke, Paul traced the outline of these muscle groups on Brad's thin frame, giving him a thrill so visceral Brad felt as though he might faint.

Paul flexed his arm, saying in that earnest, unboastful way of his, "See? I've been working out a lot longer than you. It just takes time to build things up."

Turning toward the mirror, Paul shucked his shirt and began to strike poses, first a front double biceps, then a lat spread, and Brad marveled at the power of him -- at the sheer beauty of his physique. Emboldened by the pure unself-consciousness of Paul, by the muscles mounding and moving underneath the surface of his skin as he pumped and flexed, Brad stood beside him at the mirror, wondering whether he could ever dare to touch him in the way Paul had so unselfconsciously touched him. Suddenly, Paul struck a "most muscular" pose, his muscles knotting and bulging hugely, and Brad couldn't help himself.

"Whoa!" he said, reaching out to touch the knotted bicep, veins popping and banding everywhere.

"Yeah, get a load of this, baby," said Paul, adding a final, devastating squeeze to the already massively pumped fibers.

He turned and gave Brad a playful hug; and, as the cool, smooth skin of Paul's body met his own, he felt a wave of emotion unlike anything he had ever felt before. He simply could not get over the feeling of Paul's skin: taut, cool, and masculine, yet soft. In that miraculous envelopment of flesh, he felt both infinite, and yet, incredibly specific and centered.

Lingering in the overwhelming sense of it, he held on probably a moment too long, but couldn't help it. It was the first time he had ever really held a man and, though he didn't want to let Paul go, he forced himself at last to back away. He felt his penis burgeoning and stiffening; yet, he could also sense somehow that Paul wasn't feeling anything remotely similar. He was aware of something deep within him being given final confirmation and, along with that, a tantalizing sense of fear and possibility: of love and pain embodied all at once. Here in this dimly lit gym, reflected in the perfect form of Paul, he knew, somehow, he'd be attempting to preserve and understand this moment for a long, long time.

TALES OUT OF SCHOOL

A PORTRAIT

———

MADISON, WISCONSIN, IN MID-WINTER, IS perhaps not the coldest place in the world, but in January, 1984, it felt that way to Brad Thompson. Brad had just come to Madison from Thornton College, a small, liberal arts college approximately six hours to the south in rural Illinois, and even though the geographical distance between the two places was not exceptionally great, in other ways, it was a completely separate world. Madison was situated on an isthmus between two lakes, and this proved to make it one of the coldest physical settings he'd ever been in. Regularly, the winds whipped across the frozen plains of the Midwest, continued unimpeded across the icy surfaces of the two lakes, and buffeted the soulless, high-rise buildings of the bleak and frozen, state-school campus. The change from a small, private school to a large, state one, was another shock as well. But, by far, the greatest issue facing Brad was his emerging sexuality.

Brad had only recently started to come out to friends about the fact that he was gay but, even so, his ideas about it were tentative and abstract: he'd never even come close to being with another man. Brad had been close to a few people while at Thornton, but hadn't really come out to them and, anyway, those friends were now all gone to other destinations. The smallness of that environment had always made disclosure about his sexuality difficult, and that was one of the main reasons he'd chosen such a large school to pursue his graduate studies. He was ready to get on with the business of living his life; trouble was, he really had no road map for how to do that, and the huge, seemingly indifferent, environment at Madison was intimidating.

Brad had also recently made a major decision not to pursue his under-graduate interests (Comparative Religion and Latin) and switch to an English degree, in the hopes of being able to teach literature someday. In part, his decision not to pursue his previous coursework was based upon this new awareness of his sexuality and its incompatibility with the teachings of the church. At one point, Brad had actually thought seriously about becoming a minister -- a hope his parents still entertained -- but had decided, under the circumstances, that was impossible. As excited as Brad was to be making a new start, he still hadn't communicated anything about his sexuality to his parents, beyond informing them of his switch in majors. It was a switch they attributed merely to changing interests (an assumption Brad did nothing to discourage). Brad knew that coming out to them at some point was the next logical step; but, it was a very big hurdle, and he was very nervous about how this news would be received.

Now, standing as a grad student in the midst of the nearly overwhelming population of 45,000 students at Madison, Brad felt as alone and vulnerable as he had the first day of his freshman year at his undergrad school. Already, he was questioning his choice. He had made the fairly serious mistake of not visiting Madison before moving here, and was not altogether excited about the school, the town, or the housing situation. Brad was rooming with a straight roommate, whom he also hadn't told yet about his sexuality. Brad saw his parents as a distant battlefront; his roommate, on the other hand, was just an arm's length away every night across the dingy, green-carpeted room, and Brad felt this proximity as an added deterrent to any further progress. Given the smallness of the space they inhabited together, how uncomfortable was it going to be living together with this person after coming out?

Even if it had not been for this, however, Brad had very little idea how to go about exploring his newly acknowledged feelings much further. Thornton had had absolutely no gay presence; indeed, the town itself was miniscule. Chicago had always been four hours away, but that might as well have been Mars for all the access he had to it. Brad was aware that Madison had a gay student group but, so far, he hadn't been able to gather any information about it. He was also aware that there were one or two gay bars in Madison itself, but he hadn't had the nerve to explore them, or even to work up the courage to ask someone where they were located.

One day, as Brad was crossing the quad, he saw a poster announcing a Gay and Lesbian Student Dance several weeks away. Nervous as he mustered the courage, and feeling almost surreal, he walked up to the window in the Student Union, asked to purchase the ticket, and could hardly believe how unremarkable and indifferent the exchange was. He simply could not grasp it: was it really no big deal to anyone up here whether he was gay or straight? Did it really make so little difference? Such nonchalance would have been unthinkable in the world he'd just left behind.

On the night of the student dance, he approached the ballroom warily, not knowing what to expect; yet, after all the days and weeks of anticipation, fear and excitement, he wound up being greatly disappointed. The dance was a very sparsely attended affair; very few people were there at all, and the ones who attended -- a heavily made-up drag queen who tried repeatedly to kiss him; several militant-looking lesbians; and a handful of other, older-looking and very effeminate men -- made Brad feel depressed. He'd hoped to find, at last, a place he felt at home in. Did he still not really fit in, even here? Here, where he'd truly expected to?

He left after only a short time, walking home though the freezing rain, feeling like someone all alone at the outermost edge of the universe.

In class one day, shortly after the dance, one of Brad's professors was trying to impress upon the students the essential triumph of Isabel Archer in Henry James' *Portrait of a Lady*. The class, however, was having none of it.

"Why would she return to Ormond at the end?" said one student. "She's made a mistake in marrying him: it's not the life she wants to lead. Why in the world would she go back?"

His professor -- a tall, bearded, not unattractive man -- had smiled at them inscrutably and said, "Because it's the difference between being a young, untried adult -- a girl, if you will -- and a *lady*. In other words, Isabel goes back because she accepts her fate. She decides to live with the mistakes she's made because that's part of becoming an adult. You people, being young, possibly do not understand this yet. But, you will -- or, at least, I hope you will -- someday. Part of the process of growing up is making mistakes, of course; but, an essential part of becoming an adult is learning to live with the choices you've made, and facing up to them."

"But, she can do whatever she wants," persisted another student. "She has the money."

"And yet she chooses to return," said the professor, even more smugly. "So, what do we make of that?"

Back in his room in graduate student housing, Brad was taking a break from James by reading Edmund White's newly published novel, *A Boy's Own Story*, on the sly. It was one of the first openly gay books he'd ever seen in a bookstore, and it made him nervous even to own it. He was very conscious, always, of concealing it from his roommate, and was fearful that someday his roommate might find it in Brad's stack, amongst other books by Chaucer, Henry James, and Nathaniel Hawthorne. In Brad's class, they'd also been reading *A Scarlet Letter* lately, and though Brad had read it as a freshman four years ago, this time, Brad felt as though he truly understood, for the first time, what Hawthorne was getting at: the sense of living with the emblem of one's difference, boldly visible and present for all the world to see. He was reading the Edmund White book whenever his roommate was out, and wanted very much to like it; still, he couldn't help feeling that White's main character -- while admirable in his fearless determination to lead his own life -- was so far away from his own experience here in the repressed and relatively unenlightened Midwest, that he was difficult to relate to. Nightly, as Brad hid the book within his Chaucer text, or read it as his roommate left the room to study, he felt as though he were a lot closer to Hester Prynne than to the bold and uninhibited protagonist of Edmund White's book.

Finally, one Friday night, when his roommate was going to be gone for the weekend, Brad set out for one of the local gay bars he'd caught wind of, and whose address he'd found in a gay newspaper on campus. He was astonished to discover there was a large enough gay student population to warrant an entire gay newspaper, and had kept this carefully hidden in the recesses of his backpack as well, to avoid his roommate's detection. That evening, after his roommate had taken off, Brad set out to find a bar called Rod's, located a number of blocks away from the campus, in a semi-industrial part of town.

When Brad finally found it, his impression was that the bar -- loud and modern -- was, like much of Madison for Brad so far, very impersonal. Inside the white-brick exterior, video screens were blaring music by Nina Hagen, the Thompson Twins, and Madonna and, after he had sat there, nervous and uncomfortable for a while, a man came up to him and said hello. The man was in his early twenties, tall, thin, with black plastic glasses and long, dark, somewhat greasy hair. Brad was not initially very interested in the man but, the more they talked, the less uptight he felt. After a moment, when the man put his hand on the small of Brad's back, Brad felt the floodgates open. Never before had he been touched in such a purposeful, intentional way, and everything inside him seemed to concentrate upon that one, small spot where the man's hand lay: he felt absolutely defenseless against it.

Before he knew it, they were heading to the man's apartment, where the man stripped off his shirt to reveal a tautly muscular, farm-hard body. The slight smell of beer, smoke, and sweat was still upon him and, as the man unbuckled Brad's belt, Brad felt curiously outside himself. Carefully, the man pulled down his pants, put Brad's penis in his mouth and began to suck, and Brad held tentatively onto his bicep, tattooed with the hunter green anchor of a Navy man. The man sucked Brad so long and hard it was almost painful and, as Brad stared at the anchor on the man's bicep, he reflected on how incongruous the sight of that anchor was, here in the land-locked Midwest (so far from the ocean; as incongruous as this whole scene of two men making love must be to anybody else, including himself). Brad was so scared he could hardly bring himself to move, and the man was having a hard time getting Brad to climax. At last, the man took off Brad's pants and rubbed his own erection on top of Brad's until he ejaculated. By this time, Brad was so stressed, his only thought was that he had to get out of there as fast as he could, which is what he did.

Coming home afterwards, Brad hopped into the shower, and stood for nearly an hour, letting the water rinse him clean, thinking about the night, about the sense of failure and disappointment he had about the whole thing. What was wrong with him? Why had he been so nervous? Was it still residual religious guilt, or what? Shouldn't it have felt immediately right to him to be with another man? Why hadn't he felt any of the sense of revelation and assertiveness of Edmund White's young boy -- any of that sense of finally and irrefutably coming into his own?

The following Monday, Brad was still confused and unresolved about what had happened. Coming into the dry, winter room for his Chaucer class, he spotted a man he'd often seen before in class -- the one he'd always thought was so gorgeous. The man was tall, thin, with a runner's build, and wheat-colored hair, parted on the side. His name was Neil, and he had the casual, aristocratic good looks of a tennis player from the 1920s -- someone, that is, who would not look out of place in a V-neck, white sweater and flannel pants. Today, underneath his heavy, down-filled winter coat, he was wearing a thin, blue t-shirt that read: "So many books, so little time," furthering Brad's impression that here, indeed, was the world's perfect man. Unexpectedly, Neil sat down next to him, giving Brad a momentary thrill. He'd noticed Neil the very first day, but had never managed to talk to him. Today, however, Neil looked over and said "Hi," shyly, giving Brad another weird little vibe as he'd responded "Hi" in return. Brad had always just assumed, since Neil was gorgeous and presumably straight, that he was therefore unapproachable; but, the affable, open way Neil had greeted him just now signified that he was not conceited and unapproachable -- something Brad had never even considered. All through class, he'd sat there concentrating very little on Chaucer as he speculated about the possibility of meeting Neil. After class, he mustered enough nerve to say: "I'm Brad. I don't think we've met."

"Neil."

"Nice to meet you."

They had a nice conversation that day and, afterwards, began to hang around with each other. Neil was working on his Masters' degree in English, too, though he was enrolled in a different track than Brad. Neil's section, for instance, was reading James' *The Golden Bowl* instead of *The Portrait*, and they would often compare notes about how frustrating James' style could be.

"He's just so ultra-refined, you know?" said Neil one day. "I get it, but sometimes it just makes me want to scream."

"So, is the golden bowl a symbol, or what?" said Brad.

"Yeah, I think it's supposed to represent consciousness. Each of the characters knows something about the others, or *thinks* he or she knows, but is too afraid to act on it." Flipping through his thick, paperback copy, Neil said: "Here. Here's kind of the essence of it: 'Knowledge, knowledge was a fascination as well as a fear.' In the book, everybody's always speculating about who knows what, and the bowl plays a big symbol. So, I think it's kind of a metaphor for the mind: the mind as a great, big vessel for gathering…awareness and experience, I guess."

He and Neil had many such conversations, and Brad was always amazed that Neil's love for literature seemed every bit as great as his own.

Much to his dismay, Brad discovered very early on that Neil had a girlfriend back at home, a girl from his undergrad days with whom he was desperately in love; so, there went the hope of Neil ever possibly mirroring his attraction. Still -- and again, surprisingly -- Brad often found himself hanging out with Neil and his housemates, a group of men who'd been on the track team together with Neil at their small, undergraduate college in Minnesota, and who were all still together, renting a dilapidated, Queen Anne monstrosity just off campus. Since they were all fairly athletic, Brad always felt like something of an odd-man-out at their house; and yet, they were all nice, and unquestioningly seemed to accept his presence there. Brad sensed that Neil's housemates were a group of guys who -- though jocks -- were somehow more enlightened and accepting than the norm. So, Brad felt lucky to be included. But, what he really wanted was to find a person or group of people that he could be completely open and honest with, to start living his life and become the person he really wanted to be. And yet, so far, that opportunity had not arisen.

One night, as November dragged on and a light snow began to fall, Brad found himself over at Neil's house, playing Trivial Pursuit, eating pizza, and dreading leaving that warm conviviality for the bleakness of student housing. He eyed the snow outside, and wished he didn't have to face the prospect of returning to his lonely life. As they played well past midnight and he watched the snow continue to pile up outside, Brad was suddenly struck by an intriguing possibility: what if he were to become stranded here? Wouldn't that be the perfect opportunity to confide in Neil? Brad realized, if he did so, he should probably give his room-mate a courtesy call, and yet -- irrationally -- he didn't want to do that. Didn't he have a right to live whatever life he wanted? To become, after all, the person he really wanted to be? Then, too, Brad's roommate irritated him by spending hours on the phone talking an insufferable sort of baby talk with his girlfriend, who was at grad school in California, and Brad was sick of it all. As they played on and the snow continued to pile up outside, Brad at last mustered the courage to say, "Hey, Neil, it's looking kind of bad outside. Would you mind if I just crashed here tonight?"

"No problem," said Neil. "You need to call anyone to let them know you're staying?"

"No," said Brad, feeling yet another twinge of guilt, but again, immediately dismissing it.

"No?" said Neil. "Won't your roommate worry about you if you don't come home?"

"Oh, he's at his job tonight -- he's working third shift," said Brad, lying again, though he knew not why. Once more, he told himself: why should he have to explain himself to anyone? Didn't he have a right to live his life however he wanted?

"Oh, great," said Neil.

After they had finished up the game (well after 1 a.m.), Neil brought Brad upstairs to his room, with its musty, strangely metallic smell. The bed was un-made, and the sheets were knotted in a dirty tangle in the center. Books were scattered around the room and, looking at the scene, Brad felt the peculiar, il-licit little thrill of being in this intimate setting with Neil; yet, he also felt bad. He wasn't sure why he'd lied about his roommate, and now he felt as though he was using a ruse to get close to Neil. What was he doing, standing here in Neil's bedroom, especially considering the subject he was about to broach? How could he make that kind of confession now -- now that he was literally standing in the bedroom of a man he found attractive? How was he going to stay overnight here, once he spoke out loud the words: "I'm gay?"

Suddenly, Brad wished he'd never asked for permission to stay over, and yet, it was too late to back out now. Or, was it? As he tried to decide how he might phrase his demur (*Maybe I'll just head home after all...*), Neil turned to him and said,

"You want to borrow something to sleep in?"

Brad hadn't counted on this at all and, before he could stop himself, said, "Sure."

Neil reached into his drawer and drew out a pair of long underwear. "I don't have any pajamas or anything like that, but how's this?"

Neil shucked his own shirt off, and Brad saw the well-formed chest covered with fine, black hair, neatly arranged around his nipples. Stunned into silence by the casual, unself-conscious beauty of his friend, Brad silently shed his own shirt and slipped on the slightly dingy, long underwear top. As he did so, Brad felt a kind of awe enveloping him, as though Neil himself had thrown his arms around him. He stood for a moment, collecting himself, still toying with the plan of having a discussion with Neil; and yet, he didn't see how he could do that now.

"Are you okay sleeping downstairs on the couch?" said Neil. "There's not really another bed anywhere." Neil said this as if in apology.

"Oh, sure. Anywhere," said Brad.

As they got ready for bed, Brad still wondered whether he should try to have a conversation in some way with Neil, or whether he could still change his mind and leave: he felt both awkward and upended. As Neil went up to his room and Brad took his place downstairs on the sofa, he couldn't help feeling as though he'd made a terrible miscalculation all the way around.

As the night wore on, he felt yet another pang of guilt for not calling his roommate; he'd erred in this as well. Yet, it was far too late to do so now. Brad lay listening to the sound of the heater coming on and cutting off in the abruptly, unutterably quiet, house; and still, the snow continued to pile up outside. In the morning, he would have to make some excuse to Neil and head out with all of his concerns still, sadly, unconfessed. He would have to make amends to his roommate and finally tell the truth to him; he would have to find some way, eventually, of coming clean to Neil, and also to his parents. Suddenly, he flashed back on the discussion he'd had with Neil about James' *The Golden Bowl*, that knowledge was a fascination as well as a fear. He also flashed back on Isabel's return at the end of *Portrait of A Lady*, and what the professor had said about that.

Lying in the winter-still house, alone with his new consciousness, Brad was more than ever aware, he still had such a long, long way to go.

BETTY HAWKINS

WHEN JUSTIN RAN INTO HIS old high school English teacher, Miss Hawkins, in the aisles of the Wal-Mart store in his hometown many years after his high school graduation, his first reaction was shock, then panic. It was similar to the feeling he remembered having in the past, in grade school, whenever he'd run into teachers in the grocery store or out about town: a sort of inability to believe a teacher was an actual person with a real life, the need for groceries, etc. Yet, there she was, unmistakably the same after all those years: small, stooped, with a pageboy shock of iron-grey hair that was the same style she'd worn in the late 70s when he was her student, and which was years out of date even then. She walked with the same limp she'd had then, but seemed decidedly frailer now. One of her legs had always been noticeably thinner than the other -- whether the result of childhood polio or what, Justin was never quite sure. Yet, she still charged through the aisle at one with that odd singularity of purpose that had always guided all her actions. She must have been in her seventies now and, as Justin watched her approach, he felt that same old mix of daunting fear, tenderness, and admiration he'd always felt when speaking to her; yet, there was another major issue between them that remained unresolved, and which came rushing back to him with breathtaking force as soon as he saw her.

Miss Hawkins was a literary, artsy person in the Midwest -- a notoriously difficult thing to be, especially in the middle of rural, agricultural Illinois. She taught English at the local high school, and also ran the student literary magazine, the *Rubric*, which, for over 20 years, had won the highest honors a high school publication could attain. Among students, she was known as a very tough teacher, grudgingly admired; there were also plenty of people who would simply have called her a bitch. Justin supposed the *Rubric* helped contribute to Miss Hawkins' unpopular reputation: it was frightfully literary (which, again, gave rise to allegations of snootiness), and extremely choosy about its submissions. The students in her senior creative writing class who worked on it pretty much gave themselves over to it as their only extra-curricular activity. Miss Hawkins made it plain that the demands of art were great and, at the time, Justin had been only too willing to give himself over to them completely.

Sitting in her Advanced Placement British and American Lit class his senior year (Justin actually had two courses with her that year: this one, and the creative writing course in which the literary publication was assembled), he remembered how the students -- including him -- had been complaining about Henry James' novel, *The American*, and its apparent lack of tension. He could only imagine the difficulties Miss Hawkins must have had in teaching such a static novel to high school kids. However, one particular moment stood out, because it became such a running joke the whole rest of the school year. Miss Hawkins had a nervous tic, a kind of spastic movement of her mouth and, again -- perhaps as a possible reaction to how much she chain-smoked (one student's theory had it that it was a nicotine fit, though no one ever knew for sure) -- she would often pause in the middle of a sentence, and her mouth would spasm noticeably. That day, as she talked about James' prudishness, attempting to explain it to a class of hormonally hyperactive teenagers, she'd said: "You have to remember that James probably never had...sexual relations with anyone. For him, a kiss probably was a big deal." The class was stunned, of course. Justin could still remember their disbelief: "Never had sex? Not once in his whole life? Ever?" Unfortunately, what also happened when she relayed this piece of news to the class was that her mouth spasmed when she did so.

They had hardly gotten out of the class before Nancy -- a classmate of Justin's in the afternoon creative writing class, who was not above a little parody of an authority figure -- said impishly:

"What you have to remember is, [tic tic], James probably never had [tic tic] sexual relations [tic tic] in his life."

The students around them in the hall laughed uproariously, and soon this became code "Hawkspeak:" the method of parodying anything and everything Miss Hawkins or anyone else said. The tic was always mimicked with a mouth spasm and an eye wink, so that it looked as if you were commenting lewdly on anything you felt in the mood to lampoon. The kids did it constantly and mercilessly. Justin hadn't thought it was any true disrespect on Nancy's part that led her to mimic the tic (indeed, she was a co-worker with him on the literary magazine); but, it was probably a mark of how little they understood about human pain and suffering, and how much they were willing to exploit it in their ignorance.

———•———

One of Miss Hawkins' favorite poems -- something she quoted all the time -- was a snippet of a poem by Robert Frost, called *Reluctance*:

> *Ah, when to the hearts of man*
> *Was it ever less than a treason*
> *To go with the drift of things,*
> *To yield with a grace to reason,*
> *And bow and accept the end*
> *Of a love or a season?*

Justin had thought of the quote many times in the years since, and still liked it a great deal. Along with another quote Miss Hawkins tossed out all the time as an example of a great metaphor ("Love is a bird in the fist: squeeze it too hard and you'll kill it. Don't hold onto it tightly enough and it will fly away") -- both quotes had come to symbolize Miss Hawkins for him, especially in light of what occurred next. But, like many other things, he was not to understand all that until much later.

One afternoon in his creative writing section, Miss Hawkins brought in her prize student from the year before, Jane Woodall, to read for the class. Jane had spent the summer at the Bread Loaf Writers' Conference -- one of the nation's premiere creative writing programs -- which was notoriously difficult to get into. It was the subject of legend, and universally acknowledged to be very competitive. It was also just assumed that, for those who did manage to get accepted, whatever they wrote would immediately be published. As such, it was the object of many of Justin's fellow classmates' -- and his own -- reveries, and he was incredibly excited about the reading.

Jane, appearing in a simple, shapeless, white cotton summer dress (very East Coast and artsy, they all thought), with very close-cropped hair, did not disappoint, and read poetry of stunning elegance and sophistication. Justin had pored over her entries in the *Rubric* from the years before, savoring every elegant turn of phrase. After she'd read, Justin met Nancy in the halls outside and asked her what she'd thought. She answered him in typical "Hawkspeak:"

"I thought it was very [tic tic] interesting."

"Me, too. God, I wish I could get into Bread Loaf."

"I heard they all sleep with each other -- that you can't even get into some of the classes unless you sleep with the visiting writer."

Nancy was a seeming font of knowledge such as this, and where she got her information, Justin never really knew.

"Really?"

"Yeah. I bet if you asked [tic tic] 'Miss Jane Woodall,' she'd tell you there's a whole lot of [tic tic] funny stuff going on."

"I can't believe that's true," said Justin, unwilling to let his exalted image of the place be tarnished with unseemly gossip.

"Oh, grow up," said Nancy. "How do you think half of these people get ahead?"

Nancy was a tall, awkward girl with long, straight brown hair and braces. She wasn't unattractive, but she was also the kind of girl who -- without stretching the imagination too much -- one could conceive of ending up exactly like Miss Hawkins some day: teaching English in some small, Midwestern town; an aging spinster, keeping up high standards in a place where the biggest local cultural activity was tractor pulls and drag races every Friday and Saturday night.

"No, don't *you* be so cynical," he said.

"You're a hopeless optimist, which is probably why you'll persist and get your stuff published someday, while I'll wind up jaded, bitter, and alone."

"So dramatic," said Justin, secretly pleased at this assessment. It was odd to think that all he heard back then was the part about his ultimately being published someday, while the part about her winding up jaded, bitter, and alone, barely registered with him at all.

———◄►———

Miss Hawkins had a few books she always championed in class as neglected classics of the twentieth century. When it came time for the class oral book review assignment, everyone had to pick a novel from a list Miss Hawkins had prepared, and report on it to class. Justin had heard Miss Hawkins mention a book by Pamela Frankau, called *A Wreath for the Enemy,* enough to know that Miss Hawkins held it in very high regard. Looking back, he supposed he was not above currying a little favor with her by choosing it to report on: surely, by reading it, he was being at least a bit of an apple polisher?

Justin couldn't, at this date, remember a whole lot about the book, except that it was a study of two women who were friends, one of whom went on to fame and fortune as an actress, while the other remained a trusted friend, but a friend destined to live out her life in the shadows of greatness and in obscurity. One scene he did remember had to do with the woman watching her friend -- now a successful actress -- in a performance, as Ophelia, in *Hamlet.* For some reason, he remembered the woman being particularly impressed by the way the friend had delivered the line: "I was the more deceived," after Ophelia tells Hamlet she believes he loved her once, to which Hamlet, capriciously and callously, replies that, indeed, he never had.

After he read the book, he remembered Miss Hawkins asking him impatiently, "So, did you like it?"

When he hesitated, Miss Hawkins said quickly, defensively: "It's been a long time since I've read it."

"I did," Justin replied, dissembling a bit, because, in truth, he hadn't really liked it that well, but knew that *she* had. He was also secretly flattered that Miss Hawkins esteemed his literary judgment so highly, and remembered prevaricating a bit by saying: "I'm just trying to figure out whether I thought it was truly a *great* book."

Greatness was a thing that mattered to him very much at that point: he wanted to be great; he thought Jane was great; he thought Miss Hawkins was great, and he wanted to be just like her. It was the reason they were all working so hard on the *Rubric*, the reason they endured Ms. Hawkins' difficult classes.

To that end, he and several other students from her creative writing class -- including Nancy -- were sitting in Miss Hawkins' living room one Saturday before Easter, compiling and editing the selections for that year's magazine. Miss Hawkins' home was quite a bit as he'd expected: a modest, ranch-style affair, with white carpeting throughout (she had no children or pets, so there was no fear of damaging such an impractical flooring choice). Unlike most other homes in the town, which had comfortable, sturdy sofas and chairs, and which were decorated with pictures of kids and dogs, Miss Hawkins' house had "mod" furniture: paintings and sculptures were scattered throughout, and she had an unusually large number of bookshelves. The window seats in the den (perfect for curling up to read a book in winter) had a view of a Japanese plum tree, just coming into delicate, purple blossom, in the back yard. The tree had evidently inspired her, because Miss Hawkins pulled out a poem and suddenly said to them:

"Okay, I've spent all year reading and judging your work; now, I'd like you to give me your feedback on mine. You might notice the tree in flower in back, and I'd like you all to give me your honest opinion of this." With that, she handed out some copies and began to read:

So much
Depends upon

The plum tree
Delicately flowering in the rain.

The aria from
The Messiah palls,

Lone singer's sad refrain:
The gradual

Diminuendo of
The Fall, numb

Hallelujahs of the spring,
Exalting fruit and stone.

So much depends upon the plum

Justin remembered that they'd all sat, not knowing what to say. One or two of them dutifully asked questions: what was the purpose of capitalizing "The Fall" in the one instance. Was that a reference to the fall of man? Was the reference to "Hallelujahs of the spring" a reference to the *Hallelujah Chorus?*

Afterwards -- the many hours of painstaking work of laying out the poems and getting the *Rubric* ready for publication being largely behind them -- Justin had given a ride home to Nancy, and they were gossiping in the car.

"What did you think about Miss Hawkins' poem?" asked Justin. For his part, he'd been surprised by the overall religiosity of it. He hadn't loved it, and hadn't hated it.

"Could you believe that?" said Nancy. "It was so pathetic."

"What do you mean?" said Justin. "It wasn't *that* bad."

"Oh, come on! It's so William Carlos Williams: 'So much depends upon a red wheelbarrow, glazed with rain water, beside the white chickens.'"

"Well, yeah," he said, "it's obviously a reference to Williams. After all, how many years has she taught *that* poem? But, overall, I thought it was okay. Didn't you? I kind of liked the internal rhyme."

"I don't know," said Nancy. "I feel like it's all such a pathetic attempt to mimic Jane Woodall's successes. You know, Betty's in love with her."

"Huh?" said Justin, nearly slamming on the brakes.

"Oh, yeah. Didn't you know? She takes trips to visit her at her college very often. I'm surprised she isn't there now, except we've got to get the *Rubric* to press."

Justin was stunned, not least by the insinuation of a relationship he'd never suspected, but also by Nancy's casual mention of a lesbian relationship. Since he'd long been struggling with his own sexuality, and had concluded (though not to anyone besides himself) that he was probably gay as well, he didn't know what to say. Mostly, though, he was just shocked by Nancy's characterization of the whole thing.

"I just think it's kind of sleazy," continued Nancy. "I mean, being in love with Jane is one thing, but Betty's head-over-heels gaga about her. Reading us her own poetry in an attempt to compete with her, or to be nearer to her some-how -- it all just seems very pathetic to me."

Justin was still reeling, and could think of nothing intelligent to say. Suddenly, he remembered a remark a school guidance counselor had made to him recently. He'd casually said to the man: "Miss Hawkins asked me to ask you if you could do her a favor," at which the school counselor had snapped, "I wouldn't do *anything* for Miss Hawkins. But, I'll do it for *you*." Now, think-ing back on the incident, he wondered whether the counselor's antipathy had something to do with his knowledge of Betty's sexuality -- even, perhaps, her feelings for Jane. He said, half-heartedly, to Nancy: "Yeah, I can't imagine Jane returning the feelings."

"I just think she's making a fool out of herself, chasing after her, and bring-ing her in for a reading to our class."

"Well, I appreciated having the reading," replied Justin lamely, a fact that even Nancy acknowledged.

———◆———

In later years, it occurred to Justin that, perhaps, Nancy was simply jealous of Miss Hawkins (he could never call her "Betty" in the familiar way that Nancy did); or, that she might actually have been in love with one or the other of them herself. But, at that time, he was so petrified about what he, himself, was feeling -- so locked up in his own uncertainty -- that he hadn't dared mention or explore that with her.

———◆———

Justin was to have yet one more startling glimpse into Betty Hawkins' personal life that semester -- one that would change his view forever. Looking over the proofs for the *Rubric* later that week, he'd come upon some poems he was uncertain were to be included or not. And, though it was late in the evening (about 9 p.m., as he recalled), he decided to call her. Though most teachers' phone numbers were unlisted, he had hers by virtue of his work on the magazine; yet, even as he dialed it, he felt strange, as if he were violating a secret boundary between a teacher's public and private life.

"Hello?"

The voice on the other end was slurred and sleepy sounding, and the instant he heard it, he knew the call had been a mistake: he could hear the alcohol in her voice and, as she took a second to register who he was, and he had painstakingly -- through her drunken haze -- clarified it for her, he wished he could just hang up and be done with it. Instead, when he tried to express the reason for his call, Miss Hawkins said, "Jane isn't here."

"What?" he'd said, too shocked to speak. How did she know he knew? But, that wasn't what she meant, he realized, as she continued:

"Jane isn't ever coming back."

"To class?" he said stupidly.

"To class, to my house, anywhere. She wants nothing more to do with me."

"I'm sorry to hear that," he said, casting about desperately for some way to extricate himself quickly from what he could tell was in danger of becoming a messy and embarrassing situation.

"She said she never wants to see me again -- that I'm smothering her. *Smothering!* Can you imagine?" She was shouting and ranting drunkenly, and was clearly on some kind of bender.

"I'm so sorry," he said.

"Do *you* feel as though I'm smothering you?"

"No," said Justin, absolutely mortified.

"Well, screw her. She doesn't need *me* -- I don't need *her!*"

There was a pause when neither of them seemed to know what to say.

Then, Betty said, "What did you want?"

"Oh, it was nothing," he said. "Why don't I call you up some other time?"

"Yes, some other time," said Betty, ice cubes clinking audibly in her glass as she took another sip. "That would probably be better."

He'd hung up, feeling small and scared, and somewhat traumatized. And yet, despite how much he fretted and stewed the rest of that weekend over what he would say to Miss Hawkins when he saw her at school again on Monday, neither of them ever mentioned the episode again.

———————

When he'd gone away to college at the end of that summer, he remembered consciously thinking of Miss Hawkins as he confided, first to one friend, then another, he was gay. He remembered thinking of her when he read Faulkner's *A Rose for Emily* in freshman lit., imagining Miss Hawkins, like Emily, lying all those long years in solitude. He remembered looking at his college English teacher: a tall, lean, spinsterly lesbian herself, fond of white pants suits a la Betty Hawkins, and had wondered about the starkness of *her* love life. His college English teacher lived just down the street in the small town in which he attended school, and he remembered imagining the years of loneliness for both her and Miss Hawkins -- years akin to his own: the years in which he'd lusted and loved alone, in silence, until at last he'd found a partner and the love he never thought he'd never find.

So, that day, many years later, back in his old hometown, when he saw Betty Hawkins so incongruously and unexpectedly in the aisles of the garden section of the Wal-Mart, where he was on a quick errand to find some last-minute, just-for-the-fun-of-it flowers for that same, beloved partner while he was in town visiting his parents, he shouldn't have let the moment pass to reconnect with her, and yet, he did. His senior year came rushing back to him, and -- more specifically -- that awful phone call, so that, even as he recognized that it was her, he felt so stupid and surreal, carrying some chocolates and a huge, flowering, delicately swaying amaryllis like an offering, that he'd let the chance go by.

He should have stopped and spoken; he should have told Miss Hawkins what she'd meant to him. Instead, he kept on going to the register because, you see, his gifts were meant for someone else entirely.

SO MUCH DEPENDS

———◆———

(*from the Journals and Notebooks of Betty Hawkins*)

WHEN I READ MY POEM to the kids working on the *Rubric*, they were typically a little hesitant to say what they really thought of it. It's the poem of mine that begins: *So much/ Depends upon/ The plum...*

I'm not surprised they were hesitant, and I probably really shouldn't have done that. I'm not sure what it really got me in the end: none of them is as talented as Jane was from the outset, and they likely never will be. Jane was a once-in-a-lifetime student, a one-in-a-billion person, and I shouldn't hold it against them that they don't have her natural talents.

The true question, I suppose, is what Jane, herself, would think of it, but I don't think I'll ever have that answer, because I don't really know what Jane thinks about anything anymore.

———◆———

The first time I ever saw Jane, it was just one of those meetings I knew was going to change my life. She had come to audition for the Forensics team and, even at first glance, she announced herself as someone wholly unusual: short, thin, and pixie-like, with close-cropped, black hair which she wore in a kind of Mary Martin fashion. She seemed, indeed, like some magical, little elf who had stumbled, unsuspecting, into the world. She had that fairy-like air about her of happiness, sweetness, and intelligence that you just rarely see in a human being, let alone a high school student. I suppose you could say I was smitten with her -- that's what my friend here at the school, Colin, would tell me, I'm sure. But, it's more than just me: everyone who ever comes into contact with her just seems to feel a certain quickening. Her animation and verve is infectious, and there simply is no resisting her charms.

Of course, resisting her charms is precisely my problem, because it seems like I can't. However, it seems she can perfectly well resist mine!

———————

Note to self: locate any copies in the library of Graham Greene's *A Burnt-Out Case* for class discussion. The book is now out of print, and can't be ordered from the publisher anymore.

———————

Notes for Class Discussion: talk about Greene's "Whisky Priests." The world-weary figures who populate his world.

- Greene: *A Burnt-Out Case* is "an attempt to give expression to various types of belief, half-belief, and non-belief."
- Querry - the main character's very name suggests "query," or questioning.
- He is "a burnt-out case," the term used for lepers whose disease has consumed most of his or her body.
- The main character no longer finds meaning in art or pleasure in life.
- He is a famous architect who believes the churches he's designed have been defiled by their religious occupants. **Discuss what this might mean.**
- Greene: "A doctor is not immune from 'the long despair of doing nothing well,' the same cafard that hangs around a writer's life."

———————

Today I'm thinking again -- as I have so many times since then! -- about the fiasco at last year's Forensics tournament at Illinois State University in Normal, which included an overnight stay there for the students. Situations like that, where there is contact with students outside of class, are always a risk, but especially for me with Jane, because what I was feeling toward her was so fraught with peril.

I knew Jane was preparing her Verse presentation, and had helped her with it many times in the past during the school year. When I suggested -- unwisely, I grant -- that I come up to her room (to help her prepare, of course), she gave me a look I simply can't describe it: I couldn't read it at all.

But *everything*, of course, from that point on, right up until now, depends upon how she interpreted it! The look on her face was so inscrutable, it left me totally unnerved; and, after she had shaken her head slowly and sadly, then simply walked away, I stood for a moment, still trying to interpret what had just happened; and what had not.

Then, I began to shake, almost violently. Uncontrollably.

When I was able to gather myself a bit, I went down to the hotel bar to have a drink, but I just kept thinking of that look on her face. Had she really thought I was trying to suggest that we should sleep together? We'd spent so much time together in the past, even once or twice seeing movies together outside of school and, of course, all that time spent at my house putting the *Rubric* together. But, I hadn't meant to suggest anything illicit! Or, had I? Over and over, I kept trying to remember exactly what I'd said, the *exact* words I'd used; but, even then, all of it was hopelessly jumbled in my mind. I kept wondering: if that was how she interpreted it, had Jane, at that point or ever, felt even a little bit inclined to accept? That's what I *really* want to know: if I *had* made such a suggestion at that point, might she have taken me up on it?

But, of course, she hadn't. So, that was that and, from that point on, the cards were on the table, apparently.

As I sat in the bar that weekend, thinking again and again about that look on Jane's face, I kept ordering drinks until, at last, the memory of the incident got a little fuzzier, a little easier to take, a little more charitable toward me. Even so, I had to stumble up to my room. Colin spotted me in the bar and, if it hadn't been for him, I would have taken such a tumble on those stairs! As it was, I can't even quite remember how I got to my room -- just that Colin was there, helping me.

And then, to wake up late the next morning and realize that, not only had I missed Jane's performance, but all my judging slots for the tournament as well! It was scandalous, of course. Colin tried to cover for me then, telling everyone I'd suddenly taken ill; but, who knows how many people had seen me -- and in what state? -- at the bar all night long?

For a while, after that weekend, I had no real contact with Jane: she studiously avoided me, and I scrupulously avoided her. Oh, but how I burned every day with the desire to talk to her! To hold her and tell her how special she was -- how special to *me*! If only she would have given me the word -- even now! -- I'd climb mountains for her, cross oceans, fight battles! Even if she doesn't want to have anything to do with me, she's so talented I could -- and *will* -- be her champion. If only she'll just let me!

———

Must Do This Weekend!!:

Get galleys of the *Rubric* to the printer.

Look for extra copies of *A Burnt-Out Case*, now out of print.

Empty the cat litter box!!! Last weekend, you forgot, it overflowed, and the cat wouldn't use it anymore, so the mess was all over the house.

DO NOT HAVE ANY WINE ON FRIDAY NIGHT!!! This just exacerbates the problem.

Take bottles from last weekend to the dumpster behind the White Horse Tavern and discard them there: the neighbors do not need to see them in your garbage can.

———

What the hell is Greene's book about anyway?!!! A doubting character tries to do one good thing for the world, and the world still misinterprets it and mucks it up for him. **You can't do any good in the world!!!**

Note: the protagonist is falsely accused of adultery, which proves to be his undoing, much the way I worry about being accused of improper feelings for Jane, even though **NOTHING AT ALL HAPPENED THAT WEEKEND IN NORMAL, AND NEVER HAS!!!**

Saw Glenda Jackson interviewed recently on the *Dick Cavett* show on PBS. Such an intelligent woman! So strong and fierce! At one point, she talked about how tired she'd become of late, playing all these very complicated characters, remarking that it was a relief, finally, not to have to inhabit the tortured pathways of their labyrinthine minds. Such a wonderful way to put it! I get so tired of walking these hallways of doubt and fear in my relationship with Jane. I want to cry out, like Lady Macbeth: "Unsex me now…"

Notes for Shakespeare class: *Macbeth* discussion:
  Lady Macbeth: voice of ambition or conscience?
  Banquo's ghost at the feast: real or imagined?
  A little joke: what is the name of Lady Macbeth's dog? Answer: Spot. Every time she goes to take it for a walk, she finds herself saying: "Out, damned Spot!"

In the nearly six months since she graduated, I have had no real contact with Jane. She went off to school, I wrote her several letters, but heard nothing. I was depressed, not sure how to go on -- and no longer sure I even wanted to.

  Then, just as I was about to conclude that I would never hear from her again, I received a letter from her -- a very long, very interesting, letter, in which she confessed that she'd had conflicted feelings for a long time; that I hadn't been wrong about her inclinations; but, that she hadn't been ready to acknowledge them at the time. She also indicated that -- though the dynamics of our relationship were fraught with a lot of complications -- she *did* want to acknowledge the influence I'd had on her, and hoped we could remain friends.

All of this, of course, was music to my ears. So, I hadn't been wrong in what I'd thought and felt all along! Granted, I had scared her off; but, it also validated my feelings, and actually invalidated all the doubts and fears and misgivings I'd had ever since that horrible weekend. Now, perhaps there was some hope after all!

Immediately, I wrote Jane back and asked her if she'd consider coming back and reading some of her published poems for my class. As stormy as our history has been, there is no denying her talent, and I definitely want my creative writing class to be able to take advantage of it.

Much to my delight, she has accepted, and is bringing some of her published poems to class next week. I'm over the moon with happiness and anticipation at seeing her again!

———————

Jane's reading for the class went well, but the subsequent meeting with her did not. From the outset, she was warm, but professional, and kept a slight distance. When I asked her how things were going at school, she got a very constricted look on her face, then said: "Look, Betty: I think I should be honest with you. I've met someone at school, and she and I are dating. I just want to be upfront with you, because sometimes I feel -- or at least I've had the feeling in the past -- that what you're looking for from me is something more than friendship. And, it simply can't be that for me."

I was stunned and paralyzed by this, of course: I felt a sudden rush of cold fear flooding into my heart, my ears began to ring, and I tried to act as though I was happy for her. I deflected; I disseminated, saying I was just so in awe of her talents, I merely wanted to keep up with her progress. But, inside, I was dying, and I think Jane could tell. It's a changing world, now, and I'm so envious of Jane being on the cusp of that change! Envious and sad and angry and hurt and disconsolate all at once. I asked Jane whether I could continue to come visit her at school. At first, she reluctantly agreed. After a while, however, she wondered whether that would be a good idea after all. I assured her my interest in her was simply one of admiration.

When we parted, however, there was an awful moment when neither of us knew what to do: shake hands, hug, or merely part without touching. I feinted a small hug, she leaned in for a kiss, and we ended up nearly clunking heads together. I tried to leave with as much of my dignity intact as possible; but, the whole way back, all I could think about was the awkwardness of that parting. There's a sonnet I've always loved by e.e. cummings and, as I drove, I kept thinking about it. The poem is about accepting lost love, realizing the person you love is meant for someone else, and the speaker concludes by saying that if their love is not meant to be:

Accept all happiness from me.

Then shall i turn my face, and hear one bird
sing terribly afar in the lost lands

Stumbled upon Elizabeth Taylor's (the English writer, not the actress!) superb, 1951 novel, *A Game of Hide and Seek*, recently. What an incredible writer! This story, of two people who can't quite seem ever to connect in their relationship (thus, the game of hide and seek referred to in the title) is like a little precis of my relationship with Jane.

Is this a book to consider reading for class? Would the students, at this point in their lives, understand it? Would Jane?

Took a trip to see Jane at school.
I KNOW, I KNOW -- I SHOULDN'T HAVE!!!

Still, I thought -- after Jane's consenting to read her poems at school: can't we find a way to be friends? I should have known it wouldn't turn out well. When I got there she was, of course, with her friend, and I got more and more upset as the time went along. It led to teary, drunken declarations on the quad, and I'm afraid I made a bit of a scene. The worst of it was, as I looked up during all this, I was horrified to see a fellow teacher from the school, who obviously witnessed the exchange, and who looked away at once, embarrassed. Word must have made its way back, because last week, when I ran into the school Vice Principal, and asked him whether there might be any funds for bringing bring back former writing students on a yearly basis to read their published work for my writing classes, he looked at me coolly for a moment, then said: "From what I hear, you've become a little *too* involved in your student's lives lately, Betty. You need to watch yourself very carefully."

It's so unfair! My personal relationship with a student -- whatever it may be -- should in no way deprive them of the chance to be exposed to great art and talented mentors! Still, the incident left me trembling with anger and humiliation, and I had to take a moment afterwards in the teacher's restroom in order to recover my composure.

I've decided to add Taylor's *A Game of Hide and Seek* to next year's reading list. It is, quite simply, superb. My students may not understand it now, life experience may not be rich enough for them to get it; but, someday, they will.

So, I persevere with my "difficult" readings, with the submissions for the *Rubric*, on which I absolutely refuse to lower the standards, no matter what people say. I'd rather publish nothing at all than mediocre work, which is why the magazine has won a national award nearly every year I've supervised it. Too bad if people don't like it! I'm there to ensure that they get the best exposure to art and life they can.

Today, a former student of mine came in with three copies of Graham Green's *A Burnt-Out Case* he'd found on a bookstore shelf somewhere down near Springfield. The book is out of print, but I'm still teaching it. I'd long ago told my students, if they were able to locate any copies anywhere, to bring them in, and I'd pay for them personally. He was a former editor on the *Rubric*, an aspiring writer, and -- as a student, of course -- broke. I could see he was depending upon me to pay him, which there was no question of my doing. Having to pay him cash for the books actually couldn't have come at a worse time for me, however: I'd wanted to save some funds to make another trip to Iowa City at some point, to see whether I could find a way of mending the fences with Jane. Naturally, I paid the eager young boy for the books: they were in pristine condition, we're short on copies (there are, of course, no extra school funds available for this), so what can you do?

Life is short and trying; and the pursuit of art comes very dear.

FRAGMENTS FROM AN
UNIDENTIFIED TRAGEDY

———

THE FIRST TIME COLIN BRATSCH saw the new transfer student, Dan Hutton, entering his drowsy, dispirited, third-year Latin classroom in Moline, Illinois, he sensed that something was about to change. Colin had been struggling to elicit any kind of response at all from his students, trying to convince them of Latin's ultimate rewards -- even charms ("You have to keep thinking about the verb at the end," he'd said to them. "You don't know what the verb is, and how that will affect things. Isn't it thrilling? You're working toward a word that could change everything!"), but was not having much luck. Dan was wearing clean, new, Hush Puppy shoes, a crisply starched, white, button-down dress shirt and, with the beautiful, bright flush in his cheeks, looked for all the world like a modern day Antinous striding right out of the pages of the textbook: a vision, that is, of something precious and long dead, suddenly and inexplicably brought back to life.

The new student, Dan, was tall and athletic-looking, and his skin was remarkably clear. He had fine, brown hair hanging down into his eyes and, inwardly, Colin had to stop himself from reaching over to brush it out of his eyes. Intriguingly, too, he had a single, long earring dangling from his earlobe. Dan walked in, handed Colin his paperwork and sat down. After reviewing it, Colin immediately sensed that Dan was going to be ostracized: Dan was transferring from the local Catholic school, and his transcript hinted that he was destined for something other than the norm for students in this medium-sized, Midwestern town, who mostly seemed destined for (and, sadly, contented with) Blackhawk College, Illinois State University, or -- occasionally -- The University of Illinois. Dan, however, seemed different: he had already had four years of Latin at his previous school, and was enrolling in second year German as well -- a subject Colin also taught, but was somehow never as comfortable expressing himself in as Latin. Colin could hear his students now: "He's such a brainiac: he's taking Latin independent study, *and* he's taking German. Why would anybody take *two* languages?" Obviously, Dan was taking Latin for the reason most people did, since it had informed so much of English, and German because it was non-Romance based. Between them, he was capturing the foundations of both major language groups of the Western world; he was only lacking Greek to completely round off a classical education.

Because he didn't want to embarrass Dan or ostracize him even more, Colin waited until after that day's class to speak with him. He caught him just as Dan was about to leave, packing up his things neatly into a nice, sturdy, Eddie Bauer bag. Everything about Dan, in fact, seemed clean, compact, and well-made.

"So, what brings you to Moline High School? You've been going to St. Ignatius?" said Colin. St. Ignatius was the local, private, Catholic school.

"Yeah, my mom and dad got divorced, and I'm living with my mom now."

"I see. And you're a senior?"

"Yes."

"Well, your transcript is impressive. What are your college plans?"

"I'd like to see if I could get into Harvard or Yale."

"I see. Impressive again. To study what?"

"I'd like to be a doctor."

"Terrific. That's why you're taking both Latin and German?"

"No, I just like languages."

"Terrific, so do I," said Colin, impressed again. *What a charming young man!* he thought. *Nice looking and intelligent.* "As you saw, we're working on the *The Aeneid*, though it seems you're probably more advanced than my other students."

Dan looked embarrassed and uncomfortable, his brown eyes looking momentarily (and heart-breakingly) scared. He said shyly, "I've already done a lot of *The Aeneid*. I'm wondering if we could maybe branch out into...other things."

"Such as what?"

"Ovid, or maybe some Lucretius."

Colin was taken aback. "Which works were you thinking of, specifically?"

"I don't know, maybe *De Rerum Natura*." Here again, Dan looked nervous, but it was a nervousness mixed with confidence -- even a slight defiance.

Colin was stunned: Lucretius' *On the Nature of Things* was one of his favorite works, the work of a brilliant and inquisitive mind, reaching out across the ages as it tried to piece things together and understand the world. "Okay," said Colin slowly. "Impressive. Any reason you want to tackle that work in particular?"

"I don't know. I've just heard it's good."

"Well, you've got that right. It's one of the essential texts of Western literature," Colin said. Still, he hesitated. Here was a Latin teacher's dream: a student who was enthusiastic enough to pursue work outside the classroom, whose knowledge of Latin texts was surprising -- even startling. But, was he making too much of it? Then again, how could he really be? After all, this was the first time in nearly 30 years he'd ever had anyone show an interest like this. Still, he was nervous about what implications he might face for deviating from the usual curriculum. After a moment, he said, "All right, I'll make you a deal. You help us in class with *The Aeneid* and, if you like, you can work on some independent translations of *De Rerum*. But, they'll have to be extra credit, and you'll have to prove you've also mastered the Virgil. Deal?"

"Deal," said Dan with a look of such youthful enthusiasm that -- had he not been halfway there already -- would have completely stolen Colin's heart.

———◆———

For Colin Bratsch, being an intellectual in the Midwest -- let alone a specialist in a dead language -- was not an easy thing, and he often speculated about why the Midwest, in particular, seemed hostile to the intellect. He suspected it was still a remnant of its farming past, when -- historically -- any time spent away from the fields was viewed as time wasted. Just recently, he'd come across a passage in a book, written about America at the end of the 18th century, that summed it all up perfectly:

We want hands…more than heads. The most intimate acquaintance with the classics will not remove our oaks; nor a taste for the *Georgics* cultivate our lands. Many of our young people are knocking their heads against *The Iliad*, who should employ their hands in clearing our swamps and draining our marshes. Others are musing, in cogitation profound, on the arrangement of a syllogism, while they ought to be guiding the tail of a plow.

To Colin, the quote was the essence of America's anti-intellectualism, and he ran up against remnants of it every day. Unfortunately now, of course, almost no one anywhere was knocking his or her head up against the classics, but here he was. Even the city of Moline -- once the "Farm Implement Capital of the World" by virtue of its major John Deere, Caterpillar, and International Harvester facilities -- wasn't what it once was. With the loss of many of Moline's jobs to Mexico or overseas in the early 80s, he was seeing his students become increasingly blue collar: trucks and mud-caked boots and country western stations had, over the years, edged out the Audis, classical music stations, and topsiders of all the children of the former John Deere executives. He guessed he should be thankful that the school still offered Latin anymore at all: indeed, the Latin students here were always a mere handful, even in this student body of nearly 2500. He and his students were like a small clique banded together against the tide of darkness and change that was happening all around.

The next day after class -- after, that is, his students had slogged their way through the requisite passages of *The Aeneid* -- Dan was there, all eager again, his translations written out on lined, spiral-bound paper, the tattered, curlicued edges mimicking the way his locks curled around his warm brown eyes.

As the other students left and Dan approached Colin, he said nervously, "I have some lines to show you. I figured you wouldn't mind if I started right in."

"No," said Colin. "As long as you can keep up. I admire your initiative! So, let's see what you've got." He turned to the sheet of paper Dan now shyly offered him:

Mother of Aeneas, wonderful and divine to men --
nourishing Venus -- by whose heavenly sign men navigate
the seas; who fills the earth with fruits;
by you, all living things are born and see the light of the sun.
You, goddess: the winds flee from you,
the clouds of heaven flee your arrival;
for you, the charming, artfully-made earth produces flowers;
for you, the vast expanses of the level ocean laugh,
and calm glows the diffuse light of heaven.
For, as soon as the outward face of day is brought to light,
unlocking the flourishing west wind,
the first birds proclaim you, goddess,
and your power pierces their hearts. From that same source,
wild animals gambol about for fodder happily,
and swim across swift rivers; in this way,
each captive of your charms eagerly follows you.
Then, through seas and mountains, running rivers,
leafy homes of birds and verdant plains --
in order that they may eagerly propagate their kind --
all are struck with love's arrows.

"Not bad," said Colin, impressed, but unwilling to concede too much just yet. "Not bad at all."

"Thanks."

Colin stood looking at Dan, still amazed that such a student had walked into his life. Not knowing what else to say, he said, "Let me know when you have something else for me to see."

"Okay. Thanks, Mr. Bratsch," said Dan, smiling at him winningly, then trudging off.

Dan's smile was both amused and conspiratorial, and implied a bond between them that made something long-suppressed leap up inside Colin. Being gay, Colin had never married. Of course, over the years he'd had to pay strict attention to his feelings toward his students, who'd always functioned as substitute children for him. He'd always had to monitor every interchange and interaction with them strictly, in order to make certain he wasn't crossing any lines, or giving any indication of anything untoward. He'd made a few mistakes early on: in his first few years of teaching, he'd had a number of students who quickly became favorites, and during the course of things like language club car washes or state testing events, when the opportunity arose for socializing outside of school, or having them over to his home, he'd quickly realized how fraught with peril those situations could become for him. Much as Colin would have loved to interact with those students in another way outside the classroom, the risks and potential for disaster were simply too great, and he had studiously avoided them over the years, in favor of a kind of warm, avuncular, (i.e., self-consciously asexual) demeanor. He had always rigidly stuck to his guns on that; and yet, as he watched Dan leave the classroom and thought again about that smile, he felt his heart being tugged in a new and completely different way. He was, indeed, going to have to monitor that very closely.

———◆———

The next day after class, there was Dan again, all shy eagerness, offering forth his piece of paper.

"Ah, some more lines? Good," said Colin, secretly delighted.

"Just a short passage. This one was a bit more difficult." Dan hesitated, then said, "I hope you don't mind if I skip around a bit in the text. I find sections I think look interesting, and then I have a go at translating them."

Colin was actually a bit dismayed to hear this, but dissembled, not wanting to quash Dan's enthusiasm too much. "Like I said, it's all extra credit, so I guess there's no issue. Let's see what you've got," he said as he proceeded to read:

Love's the only thing that, the more we have,
the more fiercely the heart burns with desire.
For food and drink are absorbed into the members,
and settle in certain parts; and this desire
for water and bread is easily satisfied.

From mankind's beautifully colored faces, however,
nothing is given to the body besides thin images,
and those paltry visions are often dragged off by the wind.
As when, for example, a man seeks to drink in dreams thirstily,
and liquid is not found to quench the flames that take possession
of his members, but he seeks the image of water --
struggling uselessly -- and in the middle of a raging river
thirsts while drinking; so in love, Venus deludes lovers with simulacra.

"Oh, excellent," said Colin, nearly overwhelmed, not only by the forgotten beauty of the passage, but also by the maturity of Dan's translation. I love your use of the word "simulacra" there. It's a great example of using the original root of the English word in order to give a true sense of the Latin original."

Beaming, he reached out unthinkingly and touched Dan lightly on the shoulder, then flinched, withdrawing his hand immediately, and looking guiltily toward the door as he did so. What was he doing? This was exactly the sort of thing that could get him into trouble!

But, Dan didn't flinch -- hadn't seemed to mind at all, in fact. Indeed, he merely folded the piece of paper back up and said, in that charmingly shy way, "Okay. Thanks, Mr. Bratsch," and then was gone once more.

———◆———

At home that evening, however, Colin thought again about the perils of that touch. In many ways, it was a huge risk for him to be working with such a bright, attractive young student. His friend, Betty Hawkins -- an AP English teacher he'd bonded with over the years -- had once bluntly told him: "I make it a point never to be in a room with a student, of either sex, alone." Betty -- herself a closeted lesbian -- had once fallen in love with a former student, and the situation had been messy. He'd only been able to gather little bits and pieces, but he knew enough to know that it was not a mistake he wanted to make himself. Over the years, he and Betty, by way of a mutual (though tacit) agreement, had operated essentially as each other's beards, attending school functions and dances together, and even an occasional dinner or movie outside of school. They shared a common interest in the arts, a common attraction to the same sex but, mostly, a common desire to keep the questions about their solitary status at a minimum. Appearing together for so long had given them an innocuous visibility that he supposed fooled no one; and yet, he guessed he must have decided, at some point, that this was more desirable than the scary scenario of declaring who he was, and then facing the fallout alone.

Thinking back to his college years, Colin realized that, even then, when he might have had at least a little leeway to experiment, he'd systematically avoided all contact with others, and tamped down his urges. He had, seemingly always, preferred to operate as a kind of monk, habituating the library, the study carrels, and avoiding his parents' probing questions about relationships by stating that he had his work to keep him company. He remembered, of course, being attracted to this or that boy and, in particular, to one shy, quiet, athletic boy on his floor freshman year. But, he also remembered it was almost a relief to have learned that the boy wasn't gay.

Yet, ironically, hadn't the fact that the boy was unavailable made him, perhaps, even *more* alluring? Had Colin, in a way, been punishing himself for his feelings by falling for someone who could never reciprocate his affections, creating, in effect, the perfect lover -- one who, like Hadrian's dead lover, Antinous, was not flesh and blood, and who could, thus, never disappoint? In a way, thought Colin, all these years, he'd actually operated as a kind of reverse Hadrian: instead of erecting, as Hadrian had, statues of his dead love in an attempt to bring him -- if only fleetingly -- back to life, he'd spent his days creating monuments to lovers who had never lived, whom he was *glad*, in fact, had not been real. Whatever the truth, it seemed that, at some point, he'd dug a hole for himself from which he now felt powerless to escape. Even when Colin's parents had passed away, when it might have seemed natural for him to emerge a bit from the chrysalis he'd spun for himself, he had looked around at the school he was in -- his situation there -- and concluded that it was simply best not to make waves, and to remain where he was.

But, why had he settled on this weak lie, this withdrawn, submissive acquiescence to the prevailing culture? He, who had the benefit of knowing that, in

Greece and Rome, a person's sexuality really *hadn't* mattered? Far from being scorned and shameful, relationships between men in those societies were given the very highest status, regarded as the pinnacle of love. So, why did he continually act as though that fact were something of which he was always vaguely ashamed?

———◆———

The next day after class, without fail, there stood Dan again after all the other students had exited, looking, for some reason, more nervous today than he had the day before.

"More?" said Colin cautiously, not wanting to get his hopes too high that Dan was, in fact, the perfect pupil he'd been waiting for all his life.

"Yeah, just a bit," said Dan. "Like I said, it seems pretty obvious we wouldn't have time to translate the whole poem this year, so I went ahead and jumped right to Book IV. I hope you don't mind."

Colin was again dismayed. "I see," he said warily. "Why that book?"

"I just think it's really beautiful."

"It is. It's also fairly explicit, which is precisely what concerns me. What draws you to it in particular?"

"I just want to read the texts the way they were written, not in some ridiculous version the Catholic Church has censored."

Colin hesitated, alarm bells going off suddenly. Here was the crux of the problem: if he was seen working with Dan on texts that could be construed as obscene, the jig was up. On the other hand, he had not assigned it, his student was doing something far and above what was required, and doing it -- he sensed -- for precisely the reasons Colin had always felt similarly impassioned and upset about: the willful whitewashing of the true classical past, and its often glossed-over realities.

With the same admixture of confidence and vulnerability Colin had noted in Dan before, Dan handed over the folded, perforated paper, and Colin commenced reading:

Then those who are in the first straits of an age
when seed first wriggles in the ripening members,

seek the form of a like body,

bringing news of a beautiful face and pretty color,

which moves and excites the place much swollen by seed

so that -- as if it were done -- great rivers stain the sheets.

Reading this, Colin blanched suddenly, and said, "Okay, this is now a problem."

"I knew you'd freak out," said Dan. But, don't you see, that's just the way it was! Nobody ever gets to read this stuff the way it was really written -- it's always watered down and changed. I want to read what Lucretius and Ovid and everybody *really* wrote."

"I understand, and that's admirable," said Colin, "But, we're not here to study erotic texts."

"They're *not* erotic, they're just frank," said Dan, still not seeming impudent or mischievous or lurid, just totally in earnest.

"You don't understand," said Colin after a moment. "I have to think about what we're doing. This could cost me my job." He looked at Dan, and Dan's expression was still so sincere he felt powerless to resist. Finally, against all his better inclinations, Colin said, "Okay, let's set some ground rules. "We don't discuss this here inside the school building, *ever.* Instead, we meet in the evenings or on the weekends at the library. And, this is something you've come to me to ask advice about outside of class. Are we clear?"

"Clear," said Dan, looking devastatingly confident and vulnerable at the same time. He really was such a sweet, enthusiastic kid. How could anyone resist?

"Okay. Take this back then, and let me see it at the library this weekend. How does Saturday work for you?"

At home that evening, Colin thought over the whole situation with Dan, trying to weigh its risks and perils. Dan's interest in getting to the truth of the original texts by doing fresh, new translations actually coincided with an intense interest of his own. In recent years, many classical texts were being revisited, retranslated, and rediscovered in a fresh and newly open way. Texts that had long been bowdlerized because of allegedly "shocking" notions about sexuality were now being reissued in very matter-of-fact versions, causing a number of things to be reinterpreted and reevaluated. Not that it hadn't taken him a long time to get to this point himself. Books like John Boswell's *Christianity, Social Tolerance and Homosexuality*, published in the early 1980s, had been a revelation to him in terms of understanding just how different attitudes used to be toward gay relationships. For instance, it now was scarcely deniable that Greece and Rome were places where, apparently, it hadn't mattered at all whether one loved men or women. In Greece, indeed, it seemed to have been the *norm* for older men to love young boys -- not that Colin endorsed that model, of course. But, the evidence -- made available to him only now, as he began to think about retirement -- was overwhelmingly clear: male same-sex love in antiquity had not only been the norm; in fact, it was the *ideal*.

At the moment, Colin was reading, with absolute delight, through a veritable treasure trove he'd stumbled upon called: *Greek and Roman Homosexuality: A Sourcebook of Ancient Texts*. Here was a Latinist's dream! For, gathered together in one place, were all the ancient texts that mentioned same-sex love -- those exact parts that were so often censored because of their erotic, supposedly illicit, nature. Indeed, Colin remembered the first time he'd realized that all the men in Plato's *Symposium* were essentially lovers. He'd certainly never been taught *that* little tidbit in college (an omission immortalized so well in the movie version of E.M. Forster's novel, *Maurice,* when the students are translating aloud *The Symposium*, and the professor remarks to the class, insidiously, that they should "omit any reference to the unpardonable vice of the Greeks"). The instances of cover-up, whitewashing, and abridgements were everywhere. Indeed, here was a whole sourcebook full of such examples: Solon citing the ideal of the lover as a man who: "Loves a lad in the flower of his youth," or Aeschylus, referring to: "the holy sacrament of men's thighs." And yet, that was precisely the problem: since the texts *were* frank and unapologetic about their nature, a text like *De Rerum* was a minefield of issues about which he was going to have to be very careful.

Suddenly, Colin wondered again about Dan's motives for doing what he was doing. Was he absolutely certain Dan was gay? He had, of course, noted the earring Dan wore on his first day; but, that didn't mean anything anymore. In these days of boys wearing earrings and the whole concept of metro-sexuality, it was nearly impossible to tell who was gay and who wasn't. And yet, Colin had an inkling that the impetus behind Dan's request stemmed from just such a desire to explore and validate the awareness of a divergent sexuality within himself. What else would have prompted it? Then again, these days, who knew?

It was all so different from his own past! Colin's years of coming of age had been at the tail end of those muzzy decades when homosexuality was still viewed as a disease; when everyone was closeted; when, even to mention the subject, was anathema. Indeed, he'd never had a lover -- had scarcely ever been to a gay bar. In the '80s, there had been one single gay bar over in Rock Island, the next town over, but he just about never went there, for fear of being seen and, anyway, the bar scene wasn't really his cup of tea. There was also rumored to be a gay bar downstate in Peoria, but that was two hours away. Of course, there was always Chicago, three hours away. But, that city seemed like a different universe to him: too wild and remote. Thus, over the years, he'd merely preferred to keep to himself and stay low-key. He'd lived through the era of new openness mostly as a bystander, inwardly cheering but remaining mum, and had emerged basically unscathed from the era of AIDS. Yet now, he realized, with an increasing sense of regret, all those years when he could have lived freely and openly, partaking of a joy in life similar to that he was discovering via these lost texts, were simply gone: all the beautiful lost years of his youth.

Colin poured himself another glass of wine and thought about Dan. What a beautiful boy! The thought of him was both a pleasure and a goad. What a different world Dan had in front of him, a world in which *Will and Grace*, *Brokeback Mountain*, and a host of other similar cultural milestones made everything so much easier -- made the world a very different place for Dan than it had been for Colin. He tipped the wine glass back, thought again of Dan, and felt the slow wine burn all the way down into his stomach. Turning again to his *Sourcebook*, Colin read the following excerpt:

"His love traipsed slow, a landlubber, while yours,
Circling on swift wings, flits over the sea."

How beautiful, thought Colin. And it was just one of dozens and hundreds of such little gems in the book. The editor of the book indicated that this particular tidbit was a fragment from an unidentified tragedy. It was sad that so many of these works had been lost or obscured over time, but it was wonderful to find evidence of them here, suddenly and unbelievably gathered together all in one place! Colin had been reading through the various entries for many evenings now with amazement. How electrifying and freeing it was to read these newly discovered bits, suppressed down through the centuries by the Church, by this or that faction. Here, at last, was a chance to discover the truth about that world, and to see it with completely new eyes!

This was the world Dan was poised on the verge of glimpsing. But, Colin realized, he had better be very careful indeed about what he, personally, was responsible for Dan discovering.

All the rest of that week, however, Colin could think of little else besides meeting up with Dan again that weekend. He knew that was not good; yet, he couldn't stop himself from thinking about it. What was Dan asking him to do? Was his translation of that text -- all the work he was doing -- in a way, a signal to Colin about his sexuality? Thinking again about the day he'd put his hand on Dan's shoulder, he knew it hadn't been entirely innocent on his part; and yet, it hadn't been entirely anything *else*, either. It was neither lustful nor prurient; and yet, there *had* been affection in it. How could there not be? Here was this beautiful, bright boy, coming to him for instruction: how could his heart *not* swell with fondness in that kind of situation? Yet, it wasn't desire, either, was it? He supposed it must be akin to what a father feels whenever he holds his son, which was certainly physical, but not lustful. The kids in his class being the closest thing he'd ever had to children of his own, he couldn't know, but he guessed that it was so.

And yet, what *was* the nature of love? Wasn't it both mental *and* physical, somehow all mixed up together? Scary as the thought might be, was he, perhaps, for the first time in his life, beginning to understand a little something about the peculiar society of Greece, with its unique mixture of love and eroticism? Was he, through his dealings with Dan, beginning to understand the world of ancient Greece for the first time? Colin couldn't separate it all out and, for the first time, felt he understood a little bit more about the Greeks, who hadn't even *tried* to separate it -- who'd founded their whole culture, in fact, in that grey area where love and care and attraction intersected. So, did it really matter what he'd been feeling?

But, of course, it did -- especially for him. Then, was he on the verge of throwing his whole career away by doing what he was doing? And, what did Dan know about any of that, or care?

—■—

On Saturday, still feeling somewhat clandestine and unresolved about the whole situation, Colin made his way into the reading room of the Moline Public Library, and spotted Dan, sitting at a table in the sunlight streaming in through the tall, plate-glass windows. The light illuminated the scruffy stubble on his cheeks, and made his earring glitter like a golden question mark.

After they'd greeted each other and settled in at a table, Colin began to read Dan's translation of Lucretius' magisterial text, which he'd always loved, but hadn't revisited in years. Again, he read the offending passage:

Then those who are in the first straits of an age
when seed first wriggles in the ripening members,
seek the form of a like body,
bringing news of a beautiful face and pretty color,
which moves and excites the place much swollen by seed
so that -- as if it were done -- great rivers stain the sheets.

Wincing once more at the frankness of the text, Colin steeled himself, and read on:

That which is stirred up in us, as I've said before --
the seed -- is made strong with the age of first growth.
For many forces stir up and arouse things:
but only the power of man draws human seed from men.
For, as soon as the seed ejects, goes out from its low-lying place --
through members and limbs departs the whole body,
gathering in the place of certain sinews,
immediately stirring up the genital parts of the body themselves --

those places swell and excite with seed; and there rises a desire
to send it towards that which draws forth the furious desire.
It seeks the body which wounded the mind with love.
For everything generally falls toward a wound; blood
jets out from the place where the blow was struck, and --
if he is near -- the enemy is covered in red liquid.
Therefore, he who receives the dart of Venus,
whether hurled by a boy with girlish limbs
or by a woman emanating love from her entire body,
where the wound was received, he holds tight
and desires to unite with it -- to cast fluid from body to body;
for his inexpressible desire prefigures delight.

Colin was stunned, not only by the generally good quality of the translation, but also by the details of the paragraph, particularly the cavalier mention toward the end of the possibility that a man might be attracted to a woman *or* a boy. Though he'd read the poem in other versions, he never remembered encountering this. He stared, in particular, at the phrase "a boy with girlish limbs."

"What's the Latin here?" said Colin, almost rudely.

"*Sic igitur Veneris qui tellis accipit ictus,*
sive puer membris muliebris hunc iaculatur..."

Colin double-checked, and indeed, there was no mistaking it: the reference was to "he" (the readership in that day would undoubtedly have been male) who would be struck by love's darts, whether hurled by a "boy with girlish limbs or"... He could hardly believe his eyes. Indeed, he was speechless.

"I confess, I'm a little bit flabbergasted," said Colin. "What does your translation say?"

Dan opened a dated library copy of *On the Nature of Things*, located the particular lines and began to read: "Thus then he who gets a hurt from the weapons of Venus, whatever be the object that hits him...yearns to unite with it and join body with body; for his dumb desire presages delight."

"Whatever be the object that hits him," in his "dumb desire," thought Colin, suddenly furious. *The translator had hidden the same-sex attraction in the phrase, "whatever be the object" and labeled it: "his dumb desire." All these years he'd missed it!* He felt flummoxed, stupid, angry, and upset in some not-quite-comprehensible way. "Well," said Colin, not sure at the moment how to continue.

"What's wrong?" said Dan

"Excuse me, I'm just a bit…dumbfounded is all."

"About what?" Dan smiled at him guilelessly and, again, Colin had to fight the urge to wipe Dan's bangs away, the way a pedagogue might have done to his pupil in the ancient world.

"Well, frankly, about how matter-of-fact Lucretius is about the same sex attraction. I mean, I knew it was there in other texts. But, I didn't remember it in this one, and I'm surprised and kind of exhilarated at the same time, to see it there. See how your translation hides the sense of it in the phrase, 'whatever the object,' then labels it: 'his dumb desire?' It's outrageous."

"That's what I mean!" said Dan. "Isn't it time to stand up and tell the world what they've been hiding from us all this time?"

Us, thought Colin. *So there it was: the confirmation of what he'd been speculating about all along.* Colin decided to take a risk and make it official:

"I see; I wasn't sure. So, you're gay as well?"

"I don't like to label myself," said Dan, a bit defensively.

Colin was both relieved and miffed. He was glad for the admission finally, and felt his heart race at coming out to Dan at the same time; but, he also felt annoyed by Dan's casual dismissal of his entire generation's struggle for precisely the right to be able to use that word freely and out loud. It was like a young black person's bland indifference to the civil rights struggles of the 60s -- the ignorance of all the efforts it had taken in order to get them to this point. He felt a surge of irritation, and said petulantly,

"Well, forgive my saying so, but some of us have been fighting for the right to use that "label" freely and without taint for a lot longer than you."

"Oh, I know."

"Actually, you have *no* idea whatsoever," said Colin, now inexplicably seething. "It's very easy to pass judgment on previous generations when you know absolutely nothing about them."

"I'm sorry. I didn't mean…" said Dan, looking confused.

"No, I'm sorry," said Colin, attempting to soften his outburst. "I know you mean well. I'm just…I think maybe we should call it quits for today."

Walking to his car, Colin couldn't quite seem to hold onto his books, and felt as though he were almost literally falling apart. What was wrong with him? Why was he snapping at Dan -- this eager, bright young student, who was everything he could have hoped for: a great, shining beacon of hope? Why was he so angry and upset? He thought again about the musty book's obfuscation of Lucretius' true meaning by rendering it as "his dumb desire." It was unforgivable!

Just then, Colin froze as he found himself suddenly confronted with exactly the scenario he dreaded most: as he moved across the blacktop, carefully segregated into its bright yellow herringbone outlines, with Dan close behind him, who should Colin see but a student from his class: a meek, mousy girl named Jennifer who played quiet, but was something of a mischief-maker.

"Hi, Mr. Bratsch," said Jennifer in that totally agog way students always had whenever they encountered a teacher outside the classroom -- exactly the kind of reaction he'd always had, growing up, if he ever encountered one of his teachers in the grocery store: it was seemingly so unimaginable to anyone to think that a teacher should have a personal life of any kind.

"Hi, Jennifer," said Colin, aiming for nonchalance, though he saw her immediately notice Dan walking out of the library, too. "How are you today," he said, trying to blow through the encounter as naturally as possible.

"Okay," said Jennifer, her eyes connecting the two of them with absolute certainty.

"Good. Well, have a good afternoon," said Colin evenly, refusing to acknowledge anything whatsoever.

All the way home from the library, mildly panicked though he was that Jennifer had seen him and Dan together, and wondering what on earth the fallout would be from that, still, he couldn't help fuming about that quote, and the insidious nature of what the translator had done by hiding the true meaning of the words. Once before, he'd encountered a situation like this that was similarly appalling. Consulting a set of summaries of the classics published by the *Illustrated World Encyclopedia* in 1967, he'd come across the following Editor's remarks about Proust:

> Like the other great homosexual novelists, [Proust] was always attentive to the emotional relationships between man and man, but it did not lead him to undue distortion and perhaps it is just as well that he and the others were around to treat a phenomenon that undeniably exists and is almost always treated as nonexistent or taboo.

That casually dismissive phrase, "*perhaps* it is just as well that he and the others were around,"-- the blandly evil sentiment represented by the statement that "perhaps" it was better that Proust had lived -- had sent chills down his spine, and was exactly the same kind of offhand horror that Dan's text had perpetrated via "his dumb desire." How disgraceful! How tragic! How absolutely evil, to dismiss a whole category of people so cavalierly, or to cover it up the way this translator had done for countless generations of readers, who had no idea about the true intent behind those lines! It was not even as if the content were even being obscured: it was just completely erased. It was precisely the kind of thing that Dan could have no concept of, precisely what he guessed had miffed him so much about Dan's blithe ignorance about Colin's whole generation, and the struggles of those who'd come before.

And yet, the world hadn't always been so. The ancients had understood life and love in a totally different way. He wanted to scream it from the rafters; and yet, what good would it do? What good did knowing this now do for him? Nothing was ever going to change: that was a world long lost and gone, and all his scholarship, all his knowledge about the way things "really" had been -- all his dreamy romanticizing of the past and his attempts to keep the flame of it somehow alive -- didn't matter in the slightest, because his life, and all the hopes and dreams and struggles he'd ever had, now felt suddenly eclipsed and small.

Thinking again at home about the way he'd reacted towards Dan, however, Colin felt ashamed. Besides, what did he, Colin, know about the struggle for gay rights?

It wasn't as though he'd been a combatant on the front lines: he, with his safe little post in a dead language in a school in the middle of nowhere, and no relationship of any kind to speak of. What right had he to claim that he had any stake in the gay rights movement at all? Thinking about it, he wondered whether it was just like what the editor had said about Proust: "perhaps" it was better that he was around. Colin's whole life had been so cautious: was he, too, an instance of the phrase that "perhaps" it was just as well for him to have existed? What had he done to be able to lay claim to anything at all?

That Monday, walking into the classroom, still unresolved about all this, he immediately noticed Dan was not there. Then, he noticed that the class was almost abnormally hushed. This was never a good sign and, as he tried to put them through their paces again this morning, he could get nothing from them, try as he might ("No, see, the word is 'loquitur:' it *was* said. So what does that passive voice tell you?"). Finally, in an exasperated moment, he said to them, "What's with you all today? It's like I'm pulling teeth. And where is Dan today?"

Ron McGinty, a small, blond-haired, impish kid who was sort of the class clown, muttered: "Maybe he's still at the library," at which the class roared.

Colin blanched: fear, anger and indignation rising in him. "Well, if he is, he's putting his time to a hell of a lot better use than any of *you*." He paused a moment, staring at Jennifer, who was studiously looking at the floor. Fear seized him for a moment, then anger. Then, he said: "I think that will be all for today."

As he watched the class file out, knees wobbling, he felt suddenly panicky about what had just happened. Had he just confirmed his student's suspicions in their minds via that petulant little outburst? And what, exactly, *was* he doing with Dan? Was all his interest in Dan as innocent as he kept telling himself it was? Was he, somehow, entering the territory that his friend, Betty, had warned him about? Otherwise, why was he getting so upset?

A second later, however, he concluded that not a damned thing had happened that he should be ashamed of. Still, there was the matter of the kids. What would happen if word of his private meetings with Dan should get out? Would Jennifer go tell the principal about what she'd seen?

That evening, still thinking it over, he wondered whether he should give Dan a call. He dithered for several hours, imagining this complication and that: the ramifications of contacting a student outside of school; trying to ferret out his own motivations; rehearsing what he was going to say to Dan if he did, indeed, make that risky contact. At last, mentally deciding the time had come to take a leap for once in his life, he picked up the local phonebook, found a "Hutton" in what seemed like the right area of town, and dialed.

Dan's mother answered and, as Colin strove for inward calm, introducing himself as Dan's teacher, then asking to talk to Dan, Colin wondered again what the hell he was doing.

"Hello?" said Dan at last, shyly and nervously.

"Hi, it's me. Colin. Mr. Bratsch," he filled in stupidly. "I was just wondering why you weren't in class today -- if everything is all right."

There was silence on the other end, and Colin felt dizzy. He had a sudden urge to simply hang up the phone and run, then tried to steel himself.

"Is everything all right?" continued Colin. "Did something happen today, or after we were at the library on Saturday? You don't have to be afraid to tell me." And yet, wasn't Colin afraid of just exactly that?

"No, nothing happened," said Dan. "I just wasn't feeling well."

"We can stop our meetings if you'd prefer," said Colin gently. "There's no reason we have to go on with them."

"Why would we do that?" said Dan, as if Colin's statement were the biggest non sequitur he'd ever heard.

"Well, I just thought," stammered Colin. "It seems as though the other kids might be talking..."

"You're telling me we should stop because of *that?*"

"Well, no," said Colin, suddenly feeling both stung and confused. Dan's tone was startlingly confident and defiant. "*I* don't want to stop. I just thought that if, perhaps, you were getting flak from other students..."

"Who cares if I were?" said Dan. "I don't want to quit. Do you?"

Again, Colin felt inexplicably defensive and uncomfortable in the silence. "Well, all right," he said meekly after a moment, feeling silly. "We'll continue then. See you in class tomorrow."

Colin hung up the phone, feeling curiously chastised and small. For the remainder of the evening he kept thinking about the call, trying to mitigate the sting of Dan's apparent reprimand. And yet, all night he couldn't shake it: the way Dan's tone of rebuke had fallen on him like a judgment...

In class the next day, Dan was back again, and nothing seemed at all amiss. Colin glanced at Jennifer, the girl who'd spied them together at the library, and she returned his gaze as blandly as a cat. He still had no idea what, if anything, had been said among the students. Perhaps Ron McGinty's remark had been more along the lines of Dan being a teacher's pet or nerd, rather than implying any kind of illicit relationship between them at all? He couldn't seem to figure it and, anyway, there wasn't any illicit relationship, so what was he worried about? Once again today, Dido was still pining for Aeneas, though most of Colin's students, as usual, didn't seem to care.

"Can anyone tell me why Dido throws herself off a cliff," said Colin, looking, for a moment, at Dan, sitting oblivious in the sunshine of the room. Despite himself, Colin felt his heart give a little leap at the sight of him there in the classroom once again.

"Yeah, she's in love with Aeneas," said Michelle -- one of his better students -- in that "HellOO" tone she used for everything.

Actually, Colin breathed a sigh of relief to hear this: at least they'd understood that much.

"There are those who say that love as we know it today -- romantic love -- didn't exist in the ancient world; that it's a modern construct. People often point to Dido's suicide upon Aeneas' departure as a refutation of that notion. So, what do you think: is Dido in love with Aeneas?" asked Colin, looking involuntarily again at Dan, who now met his eyes inscrutably.

"Oh, she's totally in love with him," said Michelle after a moment. "Why would she kill herself if she's not?"

"Dude, you don't off yourself for love," said Tim Salomon, a jock on the wrestling team whose presence in the class was a continuing source of amazement to Colin. He was, presumably, still addressing Michelle, though the "dude" threw Colin for a moment.

"You don't, hmm?" said Colin thoughtfully. "Anybody else have a different take on that?" He was striving very hard at the moment not to look at Dan.

"People say a lot of stupid things about love," said Dan abruptly. "Most of them are lies. Like the way they never tell you about same-sex love. In Greece and Rome, for instance, it would have been just as likely for a man to love another man as it was for them to love a woman -- more likely, in fact. Aeneas, for instance, would, as likely as not, have been sleeping with his shipmates, but you never hear about *that*. The soldiers in that movie, *The 300* -- many of them -- were lovers. A man was thought to be *more* of a man if he slept with his fellow soldiers, and it was even thought that men would fight *more* bravely in front of their loved ones than not. That's why the military's "Don't ask, don't tell" policy was such a joke. The quote unquote "gay" version of things has been systematically watered down, hidden, or erased, by the church for thousands of years. Isn't that right, Mr. Bratsch?"

The class was as silent as space. Colin looked at Jennifer, who looked back at him blankly; yet, there was no malice at all in her gaze. In fact, for the first time in his experience with her, she looked almost curious. Feeling all their eyes upon him in a way unique in all his career, Colin said shakily at last: "I think Dan's point is that some of you should take your assumptions into consideration and not be so quick to conclude that we think about sex and sexuality in exactly the same way the Greeks and Romans did. That may open up to you a whole new way of thinking you've never even considered," he added, feeling suddenly idiotic and hollow.

The class seemed to note this with mild indifference, and then the bell rang.

As the students filed out, Dan departed the room without a backward glance, and Colin felt his knees begin to shake. Was this, then, the sum total of their reaction? Was this the outcome of his years of fear and dread, the years spent worrying about what would happen when and if he should ever broach the subject of homosexuality in his classroom? Perhaps this generation *was* totally indifferent after all; certainly, Dan seemed to be.

But, it was Dan's lack of a backward glance that was the cruelest thing to bear. How naïve he'd been to think that he was able to offer him any particular wisdom at all: Dan was already leagues ahead of him! And, to think about all his worries! Even if the students had remarked upon his and Dan's meetings together, so what? How laughable to think they'd even presume there *was* any kind of relationship. What a fool and an idiot he'd been! But, not, apparently, for the reasons he had always feared. Right now, he had no clue what was going on in his students' heads -- Dan's, or anyone's. The verities were falling around him suddenly like Greece and Rome. His legs were rubber fins.

He watched the last of the classroom filter out, and returned unsteadily to his desk, where his much-thumbed copy of *De Rerum Natura* sat mutely. The words of the title suddenly meant nothing to him. It was as if, at the moment, he were utterly incapable of translating or understanding anything at all.

BUILDING ANTINOPOLIS

———————

*H*E BUILT AN ENTIRE CITY *on the exact spot where he lost his love,* thought Colin Bratsch idly one day. He'd been thinking a lot about love lately, after what had happened recently between him and one of his students. He'd also been reading a great deal about the Roman emperor, Hadrian, and *his* great love, Antinous, who'd committed suicide in a mad attempt to add years onto his lover, Hadrian's, life. As a result, Hadrian had erected statues of Antinous throughout the empire, and had even constructed an entire town called Antinopolis in the middle of the desert, not only to memorialize his departed lover, but also, Colin supposed, in order to create a locus for his grief. Colin realized he'd more or less fallen in love with his student, Dan, though nothing at all had happened; in a way, that was part of the tragedy. He was also well aware of the situation of a fellow teacher, Betty Hawkins, who'd been hopelessly in love with a former pupil of hers for many years, to no good end. Over the long nights spent reflecting upon such sad and fruitless personal tragedies, Colin started to write the following story:

"No! No! No!" Hadrian shouted at the engineers and sculptors, those simple-minded dolts who, by their incompetence and insensitivity, indicated to him they'd never cared deeply for anyone or anything in their lives: "Can't you see that sightline isn't straight? Can't you see that, just here, beneath the left eye, this statue is completely, grossly off? That the likeness isn't him at all -- isn't, indeed, like anything human or living in the least?" How could they fail to see how little the statue resembled him, his lost, his beautiful Antinous, the shape and vessel of all he loved? And yet, he, Hadrian, Emperor of all the Roman territories, would make them see, would spread, throughout every corner of the realm, the face of the beautiful, blond youth whom he had loved. He would make Antinous' image, in this eighth century of the realm, the standard of beauty and moral conduct. He would make him the basis of religions, of cults, and of all his worship. Antinous would stand for art and beauty and love until Hadrian's last days on the earth.

From the night Hadrian first saw Antinous, it was as if he were being reintro-duced to someone from his past -- linked, as it were, to something he only just now understood. Antinous was standing in the golden light of an oil-burning taper beside a column's dark red base, his golden hair tousled, his face, in the shadows, both boyishly masculine and masculinely boyish. It wasn't even a ques-tion of when this boy would become a part of Hadrian's life: from the moment he first saw him, he knew it had always been so.

"Who's that young, faun-like creature hiding by the pillar over there?" Hadrian had said to Lucius, his faithful, as they lay around the couches after din-ner that evening in summer, the soft breezes of the Aegean blowing through the lofty, blue-patterned ceilings of the rooms. The excesses of their host had taken their toll: twenty-three separate courses had already been served -- everything from olives, dates, pomegranates, and figs, to dormice, roast boar, and squab. Now, people were nearly comatose on the divans -- all, that is, except he: he, who could never let his guard down in these situations. He remembered too well the fate of the emperor Trajan, old, alone, and paranoid, poisoned as he dined in the midst of so-called friends.

After conferring with the host and his companions, Lucius returned to tell Hadrian that the youth he'd been admiring was named Antinous; that he was a Greek; and, that he, alone, among all the other youths his age, had not yet taken an older gentleman as his lover. According to Lucius, this had earned Antinous a reputation as something of a snob, and there was speculation that he was holding out for a wealthy patron to make his reputation. Actually, Hadrian saw no cause at all for reproach in this: good Roman marriages had always been arranged so that women were united with the best families; so, why shouldn't a youth of exceptional beauty hold out for the most advantageous mentor he could find, rather than trusting, willy-nilly, to the bonds through which those gymnasium alliances were usually formed?

Later that evening when, as Emperor, Hadrian could have had Antinous sent to his room as a simple matter of course, he did nothing of the sort. Instead, he invited Antinous to join him the next day to partake in some fresh-air exercise. Hadrian had decided that he did not want to take for granted a love it seemed clear to him was nevertheless already fated: he would wait for it to manifest itself on its own, the way a fine down gradually emerges on a young boy's chin.

The next day, there was Antinous on the field, looking lean and magnificent in the sun, his body not so hardly muscled as the other dark, strapping youths his age, but exhibiting a grace and fineness which seemed to elude the others. Indeed, Antinous always seemed to Hadrian to have an elegant quality rare even among all of Rome's splendid progeny. His bones were strong and fine, but there was a touching lightness to his frame, and a tawny-red glow to his skin, which made him stand out like a prince among attendant slaves. There was a confidence about Antinous, too, that reminded Hadrian of himself in younger days -- a confidence that was still shy and gentle, but which, Hadrian knew, rested inside him like a lion in its lair.

Antinous remained apart from all the other youths that day, remarkable for the fact that he seemed *not* to be striving hard to impress him -- a foil to all the other youths, who were redoubling their efforts to throw the discus further than anyone else, or hurl their javelins higher. But, Antinous was impressive simply because he *was*; he didn't have to strive to be anything he already wasn't, and this alone intrigued Hadrian.

How many times had Hadrian imagined Antinous as he was that day: the beautiful, golden curls and soft, pouty lips; the high, hard, shelf-like chest; the snaky line of blond hair running from his navel down into his loins; the great dripping handful of his balls; the thrilling sway of his sex. What was it that he loved in Antinous better than in any other boy? Surely, other boys, that day and since, had thicker chests, stronger arms or legs, or faces just as handsome. And yet, no other youth ever charmed him as Antinous did. If it were true, as Plato says, that all of us are merely half an egg -- that we spend our whole lives searching for the other part -- then Antinous was the half of the egg that completed him.

After that day, he and Antinous were hardly ever apart again, much as their union ruffled certain feathers. Celer -- that indispensable right-hand man of Hadrian's -- never liked Antinous, of course; but, that was merely the jealousy of a lover fallen out of favor. Sabina, Hadrian's wife, never cared for Antinous either, but she was jealous of all young men, realizing they exerted a sway over him and the affairs of state that no wife ever could. Besides, Sabina never cared much for anyone besides herself. If there was speculation, at first, that Antinous was looking to advance himself through his alliance with the emperor, that suspicion was quickly laid to rest: Antinous was his constant companion on all his expeditions, military and otherwise; he was his comfort and soul-mate; but, he was never an advisor. In truth, Antinous seemed bored by the affairs of state; or, perhaps it was simply that he understood implicitly that his very survival depended upon the appearance of his disinterestedness: any inclination shown by him to offer the slightest bit of advice in regards to the affairs of state would have quickly exposed him to the vultures of Rome, and they would have torn him to pieces. Luckily, most evenings, Antinous seemed happy simply to be near Hadrian in the room, whatever the topic being discussed, or walking about the streets of Alexandria on his arm.

Hadrian often used to wonder what it was like for Antinous -- he, who had, as a lover, the most powerful man in all the known world. There were those, indeed, who whispered that Antinous' death was not so much a sacrifice as a suicide -- that, as Hadrian's lover, there was, essentially, nowhere else for Antinous to go. Did Antinous, himself, feel he had reached a dead end? Is that why he swam out into the swollen, silt-laden Nile that last, awful day alone?

And yet, Hadrian couldn't believe that was the truth: they were so much of one mind, he and Antinous. He knew what Antinous'every sigh and noise meant, and he couldn't believe Antinous' sacrifice had been due to anything but love. Oh, Antinous! What he wouldn't give to experience again one of those lovely, hibiscus-scented, Egyptian evenings they'd spent together, merely lying in one another's arms, disputing with the sophists, or surveying the wealth of the civilizations of Egypt and Greece. Though he hadn't been exposed to a great deal of culture in the past, Antinous absorbed it as readily as bread soaks up olive oil, and Hadrian felt as though he were sharing his life with someone completely and fully for the first time. Antinous was his beauty, his perfume, the spice of his days, his flower in the desert. Yet, under the sway of one of those idiotic, half-baked, Asiatic religious cults, Antinous had sacrificed his life to try to add years onto Hadrian's own. Oh, stupid, well-intentioned boy! How could Antinous think that any moment here without him by his side was anything other than death itself?

He could hear them, of course, the nay-sayers, the gossips. They said his grief had rendered him an ineffective leader; that he was so consumed by the loss of Antinous he could no longer rulq the world; that his building of an entire town in the desert consecrated to Antinous alone -- creating endless statues of him and placing them throughout his realm -- was proof of his madness, and would be his undoing. Indeed, the empire was rife with worry that someone would attempt to capitalize upon his grief, use the army to displace him, topple all Antinous' myriad, inadequate images into the dust, and thereby gain control of the state. So tense was the atmosphere everywhere in the palace that, last evening, when a dancer was invited to perform a solo at dinner for Hadrian's amusement, he fancied that she, alone, remained still, while all the rest of the schemers and plotters cavorted about *her.*

And yet, he was not mad. Even today, after summoning the high priest and sacrificing pigeon after pigeon in an attempt to find out where its soul was located, and how it exited the body; even after watching dozens of the creatures die in his hands, thumbing through their viscera, looking for any similar indication of where, precisely, in Antinous, had dwelled that which he loved so much -- even then, he did not feel like a madman. Indeed, holding the entrails of these indifferent animals, he felt saner and closer to Antinous than he had since seeing his lifeless body lying there, bloated and pale, on the banks of that horrid river. If this was insanity, what other course was rational for a lover? With what else should he fill his days, if not with an attempt to resurrect that love somehow?

Today, he was having yet another statue made of Antinous, and this one was so lifelike it nearly made him weep. He'd ordered the sculptor to apply a light coating of oil to the stone, in order to give the statue some of the sheen

Antinous' skin had held in real life. Every day, since then, he'd been able to do little for innumerable hours other than sit in rapt contemplation of it. But, no amount of wishing would make the stone move and, around it, he become like stone himself, so heavy was the grief it engendered in him.

Now, the workers were lowering Antinous' magnificent, mummified body into the tomb -- its final resting place away from him -- and he thought again about how long he'd agonized over where to place the grave. Here, in the mountains above this vast and windswept plain, Antinous' city was rising, column by column, its streets stretched out in long, broad avenues against the desert's waste. Though it might be futile; though time and fate were certainly aligned against it, what other choice had he, except to labor all his days to build this city? To create a place where both their souls might dwell together and have life, no matter in what ruins that city or his heart might lie?

***

Colin looked at what he'd written and sighed. Clearly, his story was a thinly-veiled gloss on his feelings toward Dan, the transfer student he'd more-or-less fallen in love with earlier in the year. Nothing at all had happened with Dan -- Colin wasn't even certain Dan knew how he felt towards him; still, he felt pathetic and guilty about it, even if there was nothing at all to feel guilty about. He supposed regret was closer to the correct term: regret over what had never been possible for him; regret that he'd lived his life so far in the shadows, without taking any risks, longing and loving in secret. A student like Dan had the whole world in front of him: out of the closet in high school, able to talk about his desires and feelings for men freely, whereas he, Colin, had always felt so constrained. What might his life have been life without such strictures? Who might he have become if he, too, had been able to speak and love freely?

Just then, the phone rang and, as Colin answered it, he heard Betty Hawkins' voice on the other end of the line, her slurred words indicating to him that, again, she'd been drinking. Her years-long, unrequited love affair with a former student had really taken its toll on her and, more nights than not lately, he was aware that Betty had taken to drink.

"Hi, Betty," he said warily. "What's up?"

"Absolutely nothing," said Betty, blearily. "Absolutely not a thing."

Great, thought Colin. *So, she's calling me up to discuss absolutely nothing.* He knew all too well, what that really meant was she was missing Jane, and was calling him up again to commiserate. At the same time, he thought -- somewhat bitterly: *She doesn't even think to ask what's up with me. She'd rather just wallow, and drag me into her funk, with no consideration of what I might be thinking or feeling...* "I see," said Colin finally. "Have you been drinking again, Betty?"

"Why shouldn't I?" said Betty, as if defiantly. "What *else* do I have to do? It's not like I've got anything else to do, or anybody else to do it with."

"You've got *me,*" he said, equal parts indignant about her seeming dismissal of their friendship and, at the same time, aware that he was being disingenuously bright and optimistic.

"You know what I mean," said Betty.

Colin let this fearsome sentence -- this invitation, really, to partake in her grief -- go unanswered. After a moment, his heart pounding as he resolved to take this course of action, he said: "You have to let her go, Betty. Let her go, at last."

There was a pause and Colin thought his remark might really have hit home. Then, Betty said weakly:

"I can't."

"You *can,*" said Colin. "You know in your heart it's killing you, and that it's never going to work out. You're just punishing yourself by hanging on."

"Don't you think I know that?" said Betty pathetically, after what sounded like a little sob.

"Then stop. Just *stop,*" said Colin. 'It'll be horrible for a while, but you just have to immerse yourself in something else and move on. In the end, it'll be so much better if you do."

"I'm meeting her this weekend," said Betty.

"What? Why are you..."

"It's already been arranged," said Betty, cutting him off. "She's going to be in Iowa City for a reading. She didn't contact me about it, but I saw in the paper she was reading there, and I contacted her. She didn't want to see me at first, given everything...but then, she finally agreed to meet."

"Betty, I think that's a terrible idea."

"I just need to know," said Betty, suddenly lucid and on fire with seeming indignation. "I just need to know, after all this time, if she feels anything for me. If she ever even did."

"Betty," said Colin again: "I really think that's a mistake. After all this time, do you really want to go there all over again?"

"I *have* to," said Betty, with absolute finality. "It's the only way I'm ever going to be able to live."

It was a shock, then, to find out about the accident: driving home in fog, Betty must have hit a wet patch on the road, and she and her car had skidded off into a tree; or, she'd driven into it on purpose. In the days since he'd gotten then news, he'd imagined many possible scenarios: Jane and Betty arguing, and Betty driving off in haste; Jane flatly breaking off any and all further contact with Betty, as she'd tried to, long ago, leaving Betty to drive off, drunk, careless -- even suicidal. He had played it any of a dozen different ways in his head; he supposed he always would.

As he went about his daily routine now, Colin often found himself wondering: *What does one owe the dead, or to lost love? How does one memorialize it? Build tombs, like Hadrian? Write stories?* In particular, he was struggling with what to do with his grief about Betty. He'd had the brief, fleeting thought that when he'd spoken with -- and semi-argued with -- her, that last night, perhaps he should have showed up at her house with a bunch of flowers. Yet, for various reasons -- either defensible or otherwise -- he had not. So, what kind of flowers could he offer Betty now? Flowers for her grave? Some kind of memorial to her at the school?

In a flash, just before her funeral, the idea formed in his mind that maybe, instead of donating money to a charity (none had yet been designated by a far-flung brother, who'd recently stepped in from North Dakota to handle the funeral arrangements), he could establish a writing award in her honor at the school. He'd been curious about the brother, whom he'd heard a bit about from Betty, but never met.

The brother proved to be exceedingly reserved and unwarm -- the kind of person who looked to be a principal of a school in a small town, or a bank regulator of some sort. Colin had tried to welcome him at their initial meeting. His first words to him were: "I was great friends with Betty for more than 20 years." To which her brother had replied: "That's more than I can say." Her brother's matter-of-factness about the funeral preparations more than indicated why he and Betty had never been close, and the few, subsequent attempts Colin had made to try to glean more about Betty's childhood were similarly spurned; nor did he seem to want to know much about her life in Moline. Thus, Colin had never really discussed his idea with him.

The more Colin thought about it, however -- the years she'd devoted to literature, and to making the literary magazine at the school great -- the more he liked the idea of a memorial writing prize. But, upon reflection -- and almost as a challenge to the brother's indifference -- he also decided that he needed to take it one step further: rather than just establish an award or scholarship in Betty's name, he thought it ought to be called something like: "The Betty Hawkins Gay & Lesbian Creative Writing Award." A twinge of conscience forced him to admit that Betty might not appreciate being outed in that way after her death; he definitely got the sense from her brother that he wanted nothing to do with that side of her life. And yet, he concluded now with real conviction, perhaps *that* was the duty owed to the dead, and to former love: to live your life based on the lessons you've learned from that love, and to carry them forward.

As Colin formulated this plan in his mind more and more, he hoped his plan would not distress his old friend too much, wherever her spirit might be. Ultimately, he decided it just felt right. He thought again about his former student, Dan; about his story of Hadrian and Antinous; and about Betty's history with Jane. All these sad tales! All these sacrifices!

Grabbing his keys now as he prepared to head out to the gay bar for the first time in years -- another decision that just felt right, and was long overdue -- Colin opened the door and stepped into the night, newly resolved and optimistic for the first time in a long while. *After all*, he thought, *there's more than one way to commemorate love.*

MADELEINE

O F COURSE, JUSTIN HAD NOTED the name with irony. Hearing that the vacation destination their friends had picked was to be the Apostle Islands, at the northern tip of Wisconsin in Lake Superior, and that the island itself was named Madeleine, who wouldn't think of Proust's little teacake, dipped into the cup of tea, out of which sprang all of Proust's remembrances? Who wouldn't think of it, that is, especially given Justin's history with Kyle?

"Do you really think this is a good idea?" said Justin to Drew one day, expressing, finally, the reservations he'd had about the endeavor right from the start. The trip was to be a joint vacation with Drew, Justin's partner of six years, and another couple, consisting of Justin's old college friend, Kyle, his wife, Danielle, and their two little toddlers. Another friend from college, Craig, and his wife Amy, had been set to join them, too; but, at the last minute, they'd had to back out, leaving just the two remaining couples to decide whether to continue with the plans on their own. They had ultimately decided to go ahead, especially since it had been such a long time since they'd really spent any time together -- really, not since college. That was, after all, the purpose of the trip: to catch up with each other. The trouble sprang from the fact that Justin had once been in love with Kyle; indeed, his crush on him had been instrumental in bringing Justin out of the closet, though not before a great deal of heartache and anguish had been expended delineating boundaries between them.

Since then, of course, things had changed: Justin had found Drew; Kyle had married Danielle a number of years ago and moved to a small town near Milwaukee. Justin was still in regular contact with his other good college friend, Craig, and his wife, Amy; indeed, they got together at least several times a year, and had ever since graduation. But, the contact with Kyle had stayed rather at a remove, and did not seem to have progressed much over the years. Lately, it had dwindled to cards and photos exchanged at Christmas and -- perhaps -- an annual phone call. Indeed, in discussing the trip during the planning stages, Craig had said to Justin at one point: "Wow, you know, I almost feel like, in getting together again with Kyle, I'd be starting all over again. I mean, the three of us were close in school and all; but, since then, I've heard almost nothing from him. Not that I've really made any effort myself..."

"I know, " said Justin, flashing back uncomfortably on those days when figuring out who he was, and what he felt toward Kyle, had occupied so much of his mental energy. "It was so complicated between us back then, and we've obviously all moved on. But, I still care about him, and still really cherish the times the three of us all had together."

"I do, too," said Craig. "I'm just not sure how much a part of my life he could ever be anymore."

This was the crux of the matter for Justin as well -- even the thing that worried him, in many respects. Indeed, the thought of spending time together with Kyle again -- something that had been totally Kyle's wife, Danielle's, idea, interestingly -- struck him even as a bit of a risk.

"Well, Danielle must be fine with the trip," said his partner, Drew, after they'd finally all agreed to go ahead with their plans, despite the absence of Craig and Amy. "Then again, are you sure she knows all the sordid little details about your prior infatuation?" Drew grinned impishly.

"I can't believe Kyle hasn't told her. I would think he would have *had* to at some point over the years."

"There you go. So, why worry?"

"I don't know," said Justin. "I almost feel like I'm being tested."

"Is there some reason you think you're not going to pass the test?" said Drew pointedly, at which, Justin had let the matter drop. What he'd wanted to say, but hadn't, was that he wondered whether *Drew* wasn't testing him as much as Danielle. Still, he could think of no real reason not to go.

So, somewhat against his better judgment, deposits had been made, plans had been solidified and now, he found himself heading, after all these years, to a rendezvous with a man he used to be completely in love with.

And, what *was* his aim in going? In some respects, Justin wasn't worried: he loved his partner, Drew; they'd had six wonderful years together, and shared an amazing number of interests in common, from theater, to the arts, to traveling.

In another respect, though, he was worried that love -- long presumed dead but, perhaps, just dormant -- was lying there like a dandelion seed. He'd read somewhere that archaeologists had discovered dandelion seeds in Egyptian tombs and, even after thousands of years, they still germinated. Is that what his long dormant attraction to Kyle was waiting for: the right conditions to spring to life again?

———◆———

When Justin first met Kyle in college, Justin had been a lonely, self-loathing boy who had no real close friends. His sexuality was a secret he was unwilling to confide to anyone, including himself, and when Kyle came along, it was as if the perfect solid to fit Justin's cutout of loneliness and longing stepped in to fill the gap. Kyle had been supportive, sympathetic, and nonjudgmental, and it was, perhaps, this very affability that had caused Justin's devotion to deepen -- creating, in effect, an obstacle of its own for him to overcome. In the course of their friendship, Justin had had to go first through the stages of admitting to himself that he was gay; second, that he was smitten with Kyle; and third, through the uneasy vicissitudes of trying to forge a friendship with Kyle, given the hurdles presented by the first two items.

Indeed, immediately after Kyle had graduated, there was a break in contact of several years between them, after which, Justin had eventually wound up settling in Chicago and meeting Drew. Drew was the answer to Justin's prayers in as many -- if not more -- ways than Kyle had been; and yet, there had always been a sense of non-resolution in Justin's mind as to whether he had truly gotten over Kyle. Drew was fully aware of their complicated history, and even taunted him sometimes: "If Kyle walked in right now and dropped his pants in front of you, you'd leave me in a shot." These comments always led to a certain amount of tension between them; and yet, Justin knew it was not really so much a question of whether he still had feelings for Kyle. He did, indeed, though they were of a very different nature now and, truthfully, he did not think about Kyle that often. Yet, there had been an intensity with Kyle that was not there in his feelings for Drew, and sometimes that bothered Justin. He tried to tell himself that this was actually a *good* thing -- that he should never be as hopelessly (in the true sense of the word: having no hope) in love with someone as he had once been with Kyle. He also told himself there was something about first love that people never got over. Everybody said it. Yet, whenever Justin *did* find himself thinking about Kyle and the relationship they'd had, he also realized he missed it. So, what was that about? Did he really just miss the friendship, or was it, as he sometimes feared, something more?

When they finally reached Bayfield, the main point of debarkation for the chain of islands called, so portentiously, the Apostles, Justin still felt a bit apprehensive. Each set of couples had driven up separately in their own car; the drive had been long (over eight hours north of Chicago, and almost as long for Kyle and Danielle) and now, as they parked next to Kyle's maroon Honda Accord (Justin had recognized it from a long way off) and emerged, stiff and tired, from the drive, Justin had that odd, Rip Van Winkle sense of reawakening to things that seemed very familiar but, with an awareness, also, that a great deal of time had passed. The cottage they'd rented was a Cape Cod-style, grey, double-storied house situated on a gently sloping hill that ran down to the bay. The whole town was situated on a small peninsula that extended into Lake Superior, making it resemble nothing so much as a New England seaport plunked down incongruously in the middle of the Midwest. From the parking space, they could see Madeleine, the largest of the chain of islands, wooded and pine-y, in the foggy blue distance across the lake.

Even before they reached the cottage, the door was opening and there, in front of them on the deck, looking hearty, healthy, and Disney-perfect in their bathing suits, stood Danielle, the kids, and Kyle.

"Hey, guys!" said Kyle. "How was your trip?"

Standing there with Kyle looking just as sexy and masculine as ever in his square-cut, forest-green swim trunks, his black-haired torso just as elegantly proportioned as it had always been, Justin found himself experiencing an odd kind of *déjà vu*. In one sense, it was as though not a day had passed: Kyle's body was just as beautiful and alluring as before; and yet, there was a gap somehow -- like seeing a photo of a photograph -- that put the actual physical presence of his body at a kind of remove.

"Just fine," said Justin, leaning in at Kyle's invitation to embrace him, but keenly conscious of Drew watching this exchange.

"Sorry to hit you right off the bat!" said Kyle, laughing. "The kids couldn't wait. Care to join us in a bit? I think the water's going to be way too cold, but we're going to give it a go, anyway."

"Sure," said Justin, after a moment, looking for confirmation at Drew. "Just let us unpack our things, and then we'll join you."

The water temperature had, indeed, proved far too daunting, and so, the four of them had lain on their beach towels in the sun, watching as the little ones trundled up to them: Judy in her rubbery, pink onesie, and Greg in his baggy, white suit, not much different from an oversized diaper. They watched the kids playing along the sand, Greg patting the sand hills with glee until -- seized by a sudden impulse -- he began to run off determinedly toward the water. Justin watched as Kyle loped over to scoop Greg up against that awesome chest and -- despite himself -- couldn't help thinking back to his college days, when he'd wanted nothing more than for Kyle to hold him up against his chest in much the same way.

"Isn't this great?" enthused Danielle and, not for the first time since he'd first met her, Justin wondered how long it would take her upbeat, cheerleader-y personality to wear thin. In this way, she was like Kyle's first girlfriend, Maureen. Maureen had been perky as well; it was obviously something Kyle was drawn to. Or, was he just being petty now, and jealous? *Relax*, he told himself, looking over and finding comfort in the sight of Drew. *This trip is going to be just fine: the scenery is gorgeous, Kyle and Danielle are both pleasant, and it's going to be nice to spend time with Kyle's new family, getting a sense of what Kyle's life is like these days. I just have to lighten up a bit and let thing happen. This is a tremendous opportunity for us all to renew old relationships and form new bonds, and doesn't have to be some queasy, stressful test.*

"I'm really glad we could get together and do this," said Danielle, watching as Kyle returned with Greg, who immediately proclaimed his independence by running back towards the water again. However, just as Kyle was about to get up once more, Greg fell on his face in the sand and lay there happily.

"Us, too," said Drew. "We haven't had that much of a chance to spend time with you guys."

Justin smiled at Drew, pleased that he had answered. He'd been anxious all along about how Drew felt about the trip.

"So, what do you think," said Kyle, thankfully putting on his shirt at last. "Should we head on over to Madeleine tomorrow?"

"Sounds good to me," said Drew.

"You want to just wander around Bayfield a bit tonight, then?" said Justin.

"Sure," said Danielle. "It looks like there are lots of little shops and things to poke our heads into."

"Do you mind if we have dinner on the early side?" said Kyle. "We'll have to try to get the kids down early, though I'm not sure it'll actually work."

"No problem," said Justin, noting, at the same time, however, this brand new constraint in Kyle's life -- this brand new emblem of his difference.

That evening, lying in the dark beside Drew, the vast, black void of Lake Superior between them and the now-invisible contours of Madeleine looming out there somewhere, Justin couldn't help thinking back to the way Kyle had looked that afternoon, standing black-haired in his bathing trunks. He was still such a beautiful man, still such a living embodiment of Justin's fantasies that -- even though he loved Drew -- he couldn't help feeling troubled. Shouldn't he be feeling almost nothing at all towards Kyle, if he was truly in love with Drew?

Just then, Drew turned toward him, tumid, and Justin found himself saying ardently: "Oh, yeah, climb on top of me."

"Yeah?" said Drew.

"Yes," said Justin. "I want to feel you all over me."

As Drew mounted him playfully, however, Justin wondered if what he truly wanted was for Drew to cover him up, or for Drew to crush out of him any thought of Kyle.

Waking up next morning though, looking at Drew's face beside him on the pillow -- innocent, adorable -- Justin felt as carefree as a bird. The sex they'd had last night was wonderful, he felt a very great tenderness right now toward Drew -- toward everything -- and gave thanks that his life was as completely happy as it was. All his doubts from last night were gone, and he felt reassured and confident. Indeed, the only guilt he sensed right now was that he'd ever doubted that happiness.

Drew stirred and, in his grogginess, said "BeeGee," like a child reunited with a long lost pet.

"Hey, sleepyhead," said Justin. "Wake up."

"Hmm?" said Drew, now coming fully into consciousness at last.

"You disco queen. Are you dreaming about the Bee Gees?"

"Huh?" said Drew.

"You said 'Bee Gee' just now. Are you out on the dance floor in your dreams?"

"I did?" said Drew, now looking truly startled.

"You did. So, what was the dream?"

Drew hesitated for a second, then said, "BG is what I used to call my first boyfriend, Barry. Barry Gatwick."

"Oh, yeah?" said Justin, feeling a swift, involuntary stab of jealousy, even though he knew all about Drew's first relationship. "Why were you dreaming about Barry?"

"I don't know. I can't believe I said that," said Drew, still groggily. "Now you say it, though, I know I was having some kind of dream about him -- a dream where he came back to visit or something."

Drew stretched, and it was as though, by stretching, he were attempting to wring the last remnants of the dream out of his limbs.

"I don't know," he continued. "It's all gone now."

Later that morning, they were standing, waiting for the ship that would take them over to Madeleine for the day. Drew was off chatting with Danielle, whom he actually seemed to like (they'd several times formed a little cabal of their own, talking amongst themselves as he and Kyle found themselves reminiscing). With one toddler in his arms and the other playing around his legs as if at the base of some giant tree, Kyle moved over next to Justin.

"Hey, bud," he said. "How are you doing?"

"Just great."

"It's good to see you -- good to be here with you."

"Thanks," said Justin, touched. "It's good to be here with you, too."

"It's been too long, huh?"

"Yeah. It's so hard these days. You know, we used to have school in common, and now, everything is so changed."

"It is, indeed," said Kyle, looking purposively down at his kids and laughing. "You and Drew seem happy."

"Thanks. We *are*," said Justin, pleased that Kyle had said this. "You and Danielle, too. Judy and Greg are both adorable."

"Thanks," said Kyle, looking pleased as well.

"So, your life is really different now, huh, what with the kids and all?"

"It is, but it's great."

"Well, I know it's what you've always wanted. I'm really happy for you. I'm so happy, too, you've got both a boy and a girl. That always seems so wonderful to me when it happens: one of each."

"Yeah, we're pretty blessed, I have to say. I feel really lucky." Kyle looked down at the gently drooling Greg, and made a series of bee-buzz noises in his face, at which Greg smiled, uncomfortably and delightedly. "And you and Drew? Things are good?"

"Better than I ever could have hoped," said Justin, grateful for a chance to elaborate. "I never would have dreamed all those years ago -- and after all the bumpy times you and I had with each other -- that, not only would I be here in a relationship with someone who is so truly important to me, but, that I could also still have a friendship with you. That seems miraculous."

"I know. It's what I always hoped for, actually, but I wasn't sure it was possible."

"Me, neither," said Justin.

"I've missed you," said Kyle and, for a moment, Justin thought he was going to cry. This was *so* exactly what he'd wanted to hear from Kyle all those years ago; and yet, they were past that now, weren't they?

"I miss the way things were, too," said Justin cautiously. "Though, I don't miss how sad and desperate I was back then."

"I know," said Kyle. "I know it was hard for you. It's kind of weird, isn't it, to be here? When Danielle first suggested it, I thought she was crazy, or even maybe testing out how strong our relationship was. I don't know. And then, I had no idea whether you'd be up for it. But, I'm glad you were. Too bad Craig couldn't have made it, too."

"I know," said Justin, feeling a little stab of guilt upon remembering Craig's comment that getting together with Kyle would have been like starting all over again. "It was difficult for me sometimes to know how to draw the line," said Justin after a moment. "I mean, there was such an intimacy between us at school -- or, at least, I thought there was. I know you never felt what I was feeling -- not the sexual attraction, anyway; and yet, in many ways, I felt that the three of us -- you, Craig and I -- were so bonded, so emotionally close, it was almost the same as if we *had* been lovers. Do you know what I mean?"

"Yes," said Kyle, looking vaguely uncomfortable.

"That's always been difficult for me to know how to handle. I mean, there's physical attraction, and there's emotional attraction. We talked about those issues all those years ago, wondering how you separate the one from the other and, can it ever really be done? "

"That's what I mean," said Kyle. "I know that's been hard for you; but, surely, you've come a long way from that point, right?"

"Yes, of course," said Justin, still feeling conflicted and imprecise. But, before he could continue, Danielle walked up with Drew, interrupting them.

"So, are you guys ready to experience some nature?" said Danielle.

"Sure," said Kyle, his exuberance a trifle forced.

Justin saw Drew looking at him questioningly. He smiled -- a smile meant to convey that everything was fine -- and yet, truthfully, he didn't really know whether that was absolutely true.

That afternoon, as they walked around the trails on Madeleine, Justin thought about his earlier exchange with Kyle, still somewhat troubled. Certainly, he realized that part of this was probably because he was recalling all the old feelings;

yet, they were at such a long remove -- so distantly recalled and tentatively felt -- he couldn't quite say that it was, indeed, the "old feeling." After all, he'd read somewhere once that, after seven years, nearly every cell in your body has replaced itself; so, wasn't he, really -- for all practical purposes -- a completely different person now than he'd been back at school? For the hundredth time, he posed himself the scenario Drew always kidded him about, namely: "If Kyle walked up to you right now and said, 'I've decided I'm gay,' would you drop me for him?" Despite Drew's apparent insecurity about this, Justin really didn't think that was true. Kyle had obviously exerted a powerful sexual pull on him, and yet, it wasn't as though he really felt he could have made a home or a life with Kyle. That part just seemed ridiculous to even contemplate: he and Kyle were simply too different, and wanted such different things out of life. So, as he looked at Kyle now, Justin wondered again: what, exactly, was he feeling? Desire? Nostalgic affection? Or what? Kyle was still attractive, true; he still felt love for Kyle; but, what did that really, practically, mean?

As they hiked the little trails that crisscrossed the island, seeing mushrooms, wild blueberries, even Jack in the Pulpits, which Justin hadn't seen since he was a child, growing up in the ravines around his home in Moline, Justin flashed back on his childhood, playing with a boy he'd grown up alongside named Mark. Mark was the very essence of the all-American boy: a born leader, nicely formed physically: healthy and robust. In their excursions and expeditions in the woods around their houses, Mark always made the plans and led the way, created all the rules for all the games, etc. Such an archetype of the assertive male was he that Justin still sometimes dreamed about him and, over the years, he realized that he was probably really dreaming about Kyle. Even now, though the instances were rare, if he found himself thinking about Kyle, the next night or two was sure to contain some dream of Mark, leading the way for him, or Justin lost, trying to find Mark in another city. One of the last times he'd seen Mark in reality was in junior high. They'd been playing with a piece of rope, long enough to wind around the house and, as they played catch with it, Justin had bent down to catch the end precisely at the moment when Mark, somewhere in the back of the house, had yanked the rope up fast. The resulting burn rubbed the skin of his middle finger down to the bone in a fraction of a second, and Justin still carried the scar. In a way, linking up with Kyle again was like trying to pick up the end of that rope, to grasp the thread of memory once again. Only this time, Justin wondered, would he be smart enough not to get burned?

Early that evening, getting ready for dinner, Drew said: "What were you guys talking about today when Danielle and I walked up."

"Love," said Justin, frankly. "How much of it is sexual, and how much of it isn't."

"Hmm," said Drew, suddenly serious. "And what did you decide?"

"Truthfully, I don't know."

After a time, Drew said, "Well, it seems to me you've gotten past the hard part: you've established separate lives, you're aware of each other's different sexualities. Are you saying that the physical attraction is always going to be a part of it -- that the two of you can't really be friends anymore?"

"I think we *can*, to a point," said Justin. "I just don't know what that point is yet." After a moment, he added, "In a way, I'm not even sure what our friendship is about anymore, you know? I mean, our lives are so different. What do we really have in common?"

"Let me quote that famous philosopher, Paul McCartney," said Drew: "After a while, you've heard everything your friends have to say. That's when true friendship begins."

"Profound," said Justin, as if ironically. Yet, as he thought about it, it seemed as though those words offered a great deal of wisdom. Still, that left him wondering what, in the end, it meant for him and Kyle.

At dinner, the four of them sat in the attenuated light of the late summer evening around a dining table, while the kids played on the periphery on the floor. The light had that ethereal quality of the summer solstice -- nights when the light has already lasted longer than expected, and you wonder, in amazement, how much longer it can continue. The shadows were finally beginning to appear around the edges of curtains and objects on the bookshelves as they sat down to a dinner of fresh greens, grilled chicken, and a light, white wine, sitting in a golden halo of sunlight on the white plastic table. Justin found himself staring at the champagne-colored ring around the bottle, thinking to himself: *Am I not happy in this moment?* And, after answering decidedly in the affirmative: *Why can't we make these moments last? Why can't we remember them always -- these moments with our friends, gathered beautifully and unexpectedly around the table, the light rippling around the bottle of wine as the summer night deepens outside?* Even as he watched, the shadow around the bottle was growing longer, the glow in the wine notching a bit darker, when Danielle -- whom he'd actually found himself warming to all day -- said:

"Quite a beautiful evening, huh?"

"Indeed," said Justin, taking a heaping of herbed-and-oily tomatoes from the plate. He looked over at Drew, who was sitting kitty-corner from him across the table, and gazing back affably. Kyle was sitting to Justin's left, and Danielle was across the table from Justin. He wasn't certain why they'd sat in this jumbled way, but they had. Looking at the group, and conscious of the slight risk he was taking, Justin said to Danielle:

"So, what made you decide to instigate this little adventure for all of us?"

Danielle didn't miss a single beat. "How could I not want to get together with friends who've been as important to Kyle as you and Craig? It's just too bad Craig couldn't join us as well."

Justin was surprisingly and unexpectedly touched by this. "I know," he said, feeling a swift stab of guilt for his previously uncharitable feelings toward her. "I wish Craig been able to join us, too." Yet, even as he said it, he had the immediate thought of how much less awkward this outing would have been with Craig and Amy, with whom he and Drew had gotten together regularly ever since they'd been a couple. There just seemed to be a natural affinity between the four of them that wasn't there with Kyle and Danielle. Craig had been right: there *was* a gap between them and Kyle now, a lack of new interactions with them, and -- despite how nice this trip had turned out -- it still felt a bit like they were trying to graft new growth upon old limbs.

"It's nice to be able to see what your life is like now, too." said Justin. He looked over at Drew, and Drew -- no doubt recalling their conversation from last night -- suppressed a smile.

"I didn't get to have those kinds of friendships in college," said Danielle. "I went to one of those huge state schools, and it didn't really seem that different to me than high school. I feel like you guys were really lucky to have had that small, intimate, living and learning experience."

Yes, thought Justin. *But, in the years since then, a great deal of that daily intimacy was gone: their lives had moved in different directions, away from the constant interaction and daily formation of new experiences with each other. Was that because he'd been afraid to reach out to Kyle, as he had to Craig, because of the specter of his former attraction hanging over and coloring everything?*

"Yeah, Thornton was good for things like that," said Kyle. "But, in other ways it was really limited. We didn't have the resources to be able to do things like at other schools. And, it was in the middle of Southern Illinois cornfields, so, a lot of the time, it felt like we were pretty cut-off and isolated."

"Do you still see Craig?" said Danielle.

"We *do*," said Drew, jumping in freely, as he often seemed to with Danielle. "We see them pretty regularly. In fact: they either come up to Chicago periodically, or we go down to see them in St. Louis. We always have a really good time with them."

Justin was glad that Drew had answered this, but felt unaccountably guilty again to be discussing how much they saw Craig and Amy, while the unspoken follow-up question was why they hadn't gotten together as often with Kyle and Danielle, who actually lived closer to them in Milwaukee, just in the other direction.

"And Craig's doing well?" said Kyle, with no more apparent interest than if he were asking about a neighbor, or a brother or sister of theirs he'd never met.

"He is," said Justin, who still felt very strange discussing Craig in this almost third-person manner. "Craig has a small studio down there, and has been in a number of shows, trying to establish himself as an artist. He and Amy are really happy together."

"That's good. I'm glad to hear it," said Kyle, this time with more emotion. "I'm really glad things worked out well for him. There was a time I wasn't sure that was going to be true."

"I know," said Justin, though this, too, felt like a bit of a betrayal. He wasn't entirely certain he knew exactly what Kyle meant, though he assumed Kyle was talking about Craig's previous difficulties in finding the right person. He felt vulnerable on this score himself, especially given his and Kyle's history. After all, how certain had he been that things would ever work out well for himself? He'd been extremely fortunate to have met Drew after moving to Chicago, to have hit it off with him so immediately, and to have shared these past six years together with him, forging what had proven to be a wonderful life.

"I'm glad it worked out well for all of us," said Justin, smiling at Drew.

"Me, too," said Kyle, smiling at Danielle, who reached over to grasp his hand, their linked arms forming a diagonal divide between Drew and Justin.

Justin looked at this little barrier and, for the first time, was aware that he was not upset about their intimacy locking him out of Kyle's life, but instead, that their two arms were preventing him from reaching out across the table to Drew to do the same.

"And, here we all are," said Justin.

———◆———

In the still, small hours of the night, Justin had a dream that he was driving back to Thornton, searching desperately for Kyle. Kyle had told him he was coming to meet him, he'd been on the road for hours but, suddenly, he had no sense of where or when they were supposed to meet, or even why they'd undertaken this journey back to their old school. Frantically, he tried to recall the details of their conversation, but everything was becoming confused, and he had no sense of where he was anymore.

Snapping awake, Justin realized he'd been having a dream, and only now was he *truly* waking up; that here, in the dark beside him, was Drew, not Kyle. Looking at Drew's face beside him in the dark, he felt momentarily guilty that his dream had been about Kyle. Then again, what had Drew been dreaming of the other night, when he'd called out "B G?" Had he been remembering the body of his former lover, missing him?

Suddenly, however, Justin felt all his guilt and anxiety melt away, replaced instead with an incredible sense of relief. Wasn't the dream telling him exactly the opposite, after all -- that the anxieties and uncertainties of searching for Kyle had been replaced, quite literally, with love, in the very real form of Drew?

Reflecting upon this, he turned on his side and lay against Drew, feeling the entirety of Drew's body pressing against his own. At moments like this, he always felt more connected to the universe than at any other time -- more fully at peace and centered than he could ever have imagined. It had been that way ever since he'd first met Drew way back at the party of a mutual friend: there just seemed to be a spark from the first. Down through all the years of their court-ship, leading up to them moving in together, and all the years since, he'd never really felt anything but certainty that this was the right person, the right relation-ship, and how in the world could he ever have doubted that?

Relaxing suddenly into the comfort and security of Drew's body, he let him-self drift as though he were swimming out into a large, welcoming ocean, and fell fast asleep.

———◆———

Next morning, stumbling out into the sunshine on the porch, feeling the cold boards, still damp from the evening dew, underneath his feet, Justin found Drew, sitting at the little round plastic table in the sunshine on the deck, already having breakfast.

"Morning, sleepyhead," said Drew. "Kyle and Danielle and the kids are al-ready off again in their bathing suits this morning; they couldn't wait."

Looking off in the distance, Justin could see them by the water's edge, the wooded shores of Madeline off in the distance behind them across the misty blue lake.

"Some tea?" said Drew, smiling up at him with an almost heartbreaking in-nocence and beauty. "Or, we could skip it, and go join those guys down by the water, if you want."

In that moment, Drew's face in the light was breathtaking. What's more, Justin knew, even then, it was something he was always going to remember: one of those iconic images that would always come to mind whenever he ran over his little treasury of perfect moments. Still, Justin flashed once more upon that persistent picture of Kyle, standing before him that first day in his bathing suit, and wondered again: *when you are shown a vision like this from the past -- a past right there in front of you: perfect, real, in vivid, dark-green swimming trunks -- what, precisely, do you do with that? It wasn't as though you could actually grasp it, or take up residence in that moment. And yet, what good was love or a memory if it merely resurfaced and then was gone? Yes,* he concluded suddenly, *the past could be recaptured, al la Proust's Madeleine, but wasn't it actually better to love and cherish whatever happiness you had at that particular moment? For one, brief instant, you could recapture a sensation of something long-past; but then, of course, there was no way to keep it from slipping away like a dream.*

Justin sat down purposefully, with his back toward Kyle, glanced up to meet Drew's trusting face and, after a moment, said: "Let's just enjoy the moment where we are."

ACKNOWLEDGEMENTS

—◆—

I WOULD LIKE TO THANK THE following people who have read and made suggestions about some of the stories here, including: Curt Smith, Peter Bratsch, Kate McCahill, Erin Narey, Jean-Marie Saporito, and Rachel Hyde. I would also like to acknowledge Chester Rhodes' 1986 oral history (*Lydia Forbes Memoir*), located in the University of Illinois at Springfield, Norris Brookens Library Archives, Special Collections, for some details and phrases I have borrowed for my story.

Last, but definitely not least, I would like to thank Scot O'Hara, whose input has been invaluable, and whose love, quite simply, has made everything possible.

Dale Boyer is the author of the novel, *The Dandelion Cloud*. He attended Blackburn College, The University of Wisconsin-Madison (M.A.) and Vermont College (M.F.A.). He has contributed numerous reviews to *The Gay & Lesbian Review Worldwide*. His work has also appeared in such publications as *The Writer's Chronicle*, *The Windy City Times*, and many others. He is married to fellow novelist, Scot O'Hara. Visit the author's website at: www:DaleBoyerWorks.com.